FATAL FALL

'There must be something we can do!'
Holly broke away from the others and
headed for the rocks.

It took only a second for Belinda and
Tracy to make the same snap decision. If
help was needed, the three of them could
give it together.

Then a loud cry rang out that stopped
them dead. There was a sickening slide
of loose stones, and they saw a shape
plummet down.

Something fell from the rock face. A
grey shape, spread-eagled in mid-air, its
arms flung wide, falling, falling.

There was silence. Holly felt her heart
lurch. There was a splash. Circles rippled
and widened across the smooth surface
of the lake. She sat heavily on the ground
and held her head in her hands.

The body had sunk without trace.

The Mystery Club series

1 Secret Clues
2 Double Danger
3 The Forbidden Island
4 Mischief at Midnight
5 Dangerous Tricks
6 Missing!
7 Hide and Seek
8 Buried Secrets
9 Deadly Games
10 Crossed Lines
11 Dark Horse
12 Deceptions
13 Fatal Fall

Fatal Fall
The Mystery Club 13

Fiona Kelly

Hodder
Children's
Books

a division of Hodder Headline plc

Special thanks to Jenny Oldfield for all her help

Copyright © by Ben M. Baglio 1995
Created by Ben M. Baglio,
London W6 0HE
First published in Great Britain in 1995 by
Hodder Children's Books

The right of Fiona Kelly to be identified as the Author of
the Work has been asserted by her in accordance with the
Copyright, Designs and Patents Act 1988.

10 9 8 7 6 5 4 3 2 1

A Catalogue record for this book is
available from the British Library

ISBN 0 340 63609 2

Typeset by Hewer Text Composition Services, Edinburgh
Printed and bound in Great Britain by
Cox and Wyman Ltd, Reading, Berks

Hodder Children's Books
A Division of Hodder Headline plc
338 Euston Road
London NW1 3BH

1 Butterpike Hall

'I hate heights!' Belinda Hayes moaned. She clung to a branch, her eyes shut tight. The sheer grey rock of Butterpike Fell loomed overhead. Below her feet, the valley fell away steeply. It ended in a long, thin lake, glinting blue and silver under a sunny sky.

'Hang on, Tracy. Belinda's stuck!' Holly Adams called out. She glanced up at her blonde friend's slim, athletic figure. Tracy Foster was already halfway up a rock face, scrambling ahead. With her long legs and good balance, she was made for this week of outdoor pursuits at Butterpike Hall. Tracy could climb, she could swim, out-run all the others in their year at the Winifred Bowen-Davies school. Belinda on the other hand . . . well, Belinda hated the great outdoors. She was much happier watching television and eating ice-cream.

'Here!' Holly sighed and offered a helping hand.

1

'Grab on to me. That's right. Look, it's not really that steep. You're quite safe; come on!'

'O-o-oh!' Belinda groaned. Gradually she let go of the tree and eased herself up on to the ledge of rock where Holly stood. 'Why did I ever let you talk me into this?' she gasped.

Holly grinned. She took in a deep breath of clean, fresh air. 'Because it's good for you.'

'Oh no, it's not. I'm allergic to exercise, you know that. Except riding, and that's what I'd hoped I might find at Butterpike Hall. No such luck!' Belinda opened her eyes a fraction and glimpsed the spectacular remote hillsides of the Lake District rolling away beneath her feet. She gulped and clutched on to Holly's T-shirt. 'Tell me again. What am I *doing* here?'

'OK, then. You're here because we're a team; you, me and Tracy. The Mystery Club. We stick together. That's why you've come!' Holly enjoyed teasing her friend.

'Oh, yes, of course,' Belinda nodded. 'For some reason that had slipped my mind!' She opened one eye and spotted Tracy perched like a mountain goat on a ledge twenty metres above her head. 'I must be mad!' she said, as she clapped one hand over her eyes again.

Holly laughed. Today she wore her light brown

hair in a pony-tail high on her head, to keep it out of her way. Her grey eyes sparkled. 'Think of it as a week away from it all,' she advised. 'No school, no homework; heaven!'

Belinda wasn't convinced. 'Give me a history assignment to do any day!' She peeped through a gap in her fingers. 'Oh God, how can Tracy *do* that?' she groaned.

'Hey, come on up, you two!' Tracy yelled from her ledge. 'You get a great view up here. I can see the Hall and the lake, and the village. Hey, there are boats, windsurfers, everything! It's fantastic!' Her short blonde hair was blown back, and the sun struck her full in the face.

'Maybe we should be getting back,' Holly suggested. 'We can explore again later. There's a meeting before lunch in the games room, remember.' She looked at her watch. It was eleven-thirty.

'Yes!' Belinda jumped in. 'We should definitely be getting back! How sad. We'll have to leave risking our necks for another day. We don't want to miss our meeting!' She nodded frantically and pulled at Holly's T-shirt. Her knees felt weak, her legs wobbly.

Belinda groaned as she realised that this was only the first morning of their week-long course. Fifty students from the Winifred Bowen-Davies school

3

had originally signed up for the outdoor activity course, but only thirty had been lucky enough to be selected. They were to spend their days learning river-rafting, orienteering, windsurfing on the lake and, of course, mountain climbing. The activity centre was run by a team of highly-trained leaders. Every year at this time in early summer, a group from Willow Dale came to the Lake District to enjoy the outdoor pursuits.

'We'll get into trouble if we're all late,' Belinda insisted. 'Tracy, why don't you come down from that mountain you're trying to climb?' Still she could hardly bear to look.

'It's hardly a mountain. It's only a fellside.' Tracy began to scramble back down to the level of the other two girls. 'You should see the Rockies back home. Now, that's what you call mountains!' She grinned and jumped down the last couple of metres, then stood, feet apart, hands on hips.

'No thanks,' Belinda muttered. 'Not unless they're on the TV or in a video.'

'Couch-potato!' Tracy teased. She led the way down the steep hillside, finding her footing amongst the loose slabs of grey slate rock.

'That's the nicest thing you've said to me all day!' Belinda insisted. She followed more slowly, her faded green sweat-shirt rolled up to her elbows, her long, mousy hair blowing across her face.

Holly ignored the teasing going on between her two friends to follow her own train of thought. *Tracy's right, this is great*, she thought. *No Jamie to pester me for a whole week!* She'd waved her little brother goodbye early that morning as he stood bleary-eyed on their front doorstep in Willow Dale with their mum and dad. *No helping round the house. No responsibilities.* What could be better than a carefree week of sailing and mountain biking?

As they walked down the hill into the oak woods surrounding Butterpike Hall, she felt all the thrill of a holiday away from it all, with her two best friends. 'We could do with a nice little mystery to keep us ticking over,' she said out loud. They were crossing the lawn towards the old stone house with its pointed gables and narrow windows.

Tracy's blue eyes met hers as they walked along side by side. 'Hey, yes! Maybe hidden treasure?' She looked up at the top storey of Butterpike Hall. It was set deep in the woods, and with its closed-off attics and its ancient crumbling stonework, it was good territory for old treasure hoards. The house had once been a private mansion, but was now set up as an outdoor pursuits centre run by the education authority. Many school parties came

5

here for a week of activities run by professional climbers, orienteers and sailors.

'How about a body in the lake?' Belinda put in. Back on level ground, she was more her usual easy-going self. 'Or an ancient map tucked away in one of those old books in the library? You know, a plan showing a trail leading to *buried* treasure, say!' Her own eyes lit up behind her wire-framed glasses.

'Been there, done that!' Holly reminded her. The very first mystery that brought the three girls together after Holly had arrived in Yorkshire from her school in London had involved solving clues hidden in an old oil painting. 'No, what we need is something fresh and different.' She smiled up expectantly at the lion's face carved in stone above the old entranceway.

'An undercover trade in priceless antiques!' Tracy's imagination ran on. Butterpike Hall still had its original furniture. The entrance hall had wood-panelled walls, a grandfather clock, a long oak table which ran lengthways towards what was now the games room.

'Or a body in the lake!' Belinda insisted. 'We're in the Lake District, after all. What better than a corpse, trapped in the depths of a lake for centuries? Suddenly it's released from under a rock and floats up to the surface one moonlit night!'

6

'Spooky!' Tracy said. 'A woman's skeleton with a gold chain round its neck, and a locket with a secret message to a lost love!

Holly saw that they were beginning to get carried away. 'Do skeletons rise to the surface?' she asked, matter of fact. She glanced through the long, diamond-patterned window, out across the grounds to the shore and the lake beyond.

'You have a point there.' Tracy had to admit. 'Well, whatever!'

They took their places on a bench along one wall of the games room, beside their friends from school. The snooker table in the centre of the room was covered with a beige cloth, and Jo Thomas, the head of the centre, stood arranging maps and leaflets on it. Behind her, a small group of leaders including a good-looking man in his late twenties, tall, lean and fit, stood chatting.

'Espionage?' Belinda whispered.

'What?' Holly opened her eyes wide.

'Industrial spying. People stealing secrets worth millions of pounds. Isn't there a power plant around here somewhere?'

'Yes, but that's a little out of our league,' Tracy pointed out. 'We want a mystery we can sort out by ourselves.'

Steffie Smith overheard. 'Don't you three ever

7

stop?' she leaned over to ask. Steffie was editor of *Winformation*, the school magazine. She was glad to have Holly's help as sub-editor, and took articles on the activities of the Mystery Club. But even she had come to the Lakes determined to take a break.

'No, and aren't you glad?' Holly said with a grin. 'Or else, what would you fill the pages of *Winformation* with?' She knew the Mystery Club usually provided Steffie with some of the best stories for the magazine.

Steffie grinned back. 'You'll be too busy this week learning to abseil and shoot rapids to have time to *find* a mystery, let alone *solve* one,' she warned.

Belinda shuddered. 'Don't talk about it, please!' She felt herself go pale at the thought of so much physical activity. 'Maybe I should phone home with a mystery ailment, and get taken away from this place,' she suggested. 'I mean, just look. It's packed with people wearing shorts. They've all got sturdy, brown legs and compasses and stopwatches hanging round their necks!' Two other schools besides the Winifred Bowen-Davies had booked into the centre for the week. Altogether, just under a hundred kids and a dozen or so leaders had gathered for the opening meeting.

Jo Thomas had stepped forward to begin her welcoming speech. But Tracy wanted to put in a final word to Steffie. 'Don't you believe it!' she warned. 'Out here, in the middle of nowhere in this creepy old hall, we're bound to find a nice mystery brewing.'

'Crawling out of the walls!' Holly declared.

'Shh!' Belinda warned. Then she sighed. 'I suppose it was too much to expect to have a week off from mysteries.'

Tracy and Holly laughed. They knew Belinda too well. She was as keen on following clues as they were, only she didn't make it so obvious.

'I'll hold the front page!' Steffie laughed too, just as Jo began her announcements about safety routines and activities on offer.

'Now, we're not promising you an easy week at Butterpike Hall,' she warned them. She was a tall, athletic woman with long, auburn hair and a friendly smile.

Holly heard Belinda sigh once more.

'We'll expect you to push yourselves physically as well as mentally. You'll be meeting new challenges every day. Climbing a mountain is hard work, believe me!'

Another groan escaped from Belinda.

'But we also want you to have fun!' Jo Thomas assured them with a smile. 'This week isn't only about grit and determination. It's about teamwork and sharing. It's about the buzz you get when you reach the top of the mountain. And of course we do manage to fit in some relaxation; a couple of discos, a barbecue evening, and the use of the facilities here in the games room.' She looked round at the eager faces, then finished her speech. 'Above all, we aim to make this a week you'll remember for the rest of your lives!'

'I'm sure this week is going to be the last one *of* my life,' Belinda muttered to Holly and Tracy. 'Why *do* I let you get me into these things?'

2 Runaway

'I'll give you a nice easy task for a start,' Mike Sandford promised. After Jo's talk, they'd split up into a dozen or so groups, each under one of the centre leaders. They stood outside the Hall in the afternoon sun, quietly waiting for instructions.

Holly, Belinda and Tracy had chosen to be in the group led by the tall, healthy-looking young man with short brown hair, a good tan, and an easy-going smile. But if they'd expected him to be soft on them, they soon found out differently as he described what he wanted them to do.

'Nothing too strenuous,' he went on. 'I see from the forms you filled in when you applied for the course that you all ticked the box to say you can ride a mountain bike.' He checked round the group of six; the three members of the Mystery Club, plus Steffie, Mark Wright and Ollie Swain, two boys from the Lower Sixth year at school. 'Good. Well, I want you to take a gentle little trip up the

11

fellside, using the track between these two points here.' He gathered his group round him to show them a map. 'Don't worry, I'll bring up the rear to help any stragglers. The gradient is ten per cent for most of the ascent. That means for every ten metres you travel forward, you rise one metre, got it?'

Belinda looked dazed. 'You mean we have to cycle up that hill?' she gasped. It was the track up Butterpike Fell that they'd followed for their first look round the place.

'Don't worry, we'll soon have you fit,' Mike promised. He wore a white polo shirt loose over black shorts and expensive trainers. He led them to the bike shed, where they each chose a bike and followed him on to a bridlepath.

Belinda grumbled, but she settled in at the back of the group as Tracy and Holly cycled ahead. If this was a gentle little trip, she wondered, what did Mike Sandford call difficult? Her legs were aching and the journey had only just begun. 'Why can't we just walk up nice and slowly, then cycle back down?' she shouted ahead to Tracy and Holly.

'Save your breath!' came Tracy's reply. 'I think you're going to need it!'

'You can make it!' Holly yelled encouragement.

They took the winding drovers' track up the

hillside, a line of bikes strung out along the ancient road.

'That's it, choose a low gear.' Mike waited for Belinda. 'Never mind the loose stones. These mountain bikes are built to cope. Mark, keep clear of those tractor ruts, come to the left side, that's it!'

Mark Wright, a solid, well-built boy, did as he was told.

'Tracy, you have to learn to pace yourself,' Mike advised. 'Don't shoot off in front, or you won't have enough energy left to reach the top!'

Tracy adjusted her speed. The effort of the steep climb over rough ground was even getting to her.

'That's good, Holly. You can move up a gear now. The next bit isn't so steep.' Mike kept them all going. Holly enjoyed his praise, though her legs ached and her lungs sucked in gulps of air. Even Belinda liked Mike's style and grew determined to make it to the top. She felt the cool breeze get up as the horizon of jagged rocks and moorland came within reach.

Holly breathed hard as she joined Tracy on the crest of the hill. They waited, as Belinda overtook one or two others to join them. Then they stood astride their chunky mountain bikes, taking in the view. From this point high on the fell they'd climbed earlier that day, the land swept down to valleys and lakes below. They felt on top of the world.

'Very good!' Mike congratulated them all. 'I'm impressed. It means we can move straight on to some more complicated tasks this evening.'

'Like cycling downhill?' Belinda suggested, still breathless. Her heart was pounding, and though she was glad she hadn't let herself down, she still fancied an evening activity that was a little easier on the legs.

Mike tutted. 'You're not giving in, are you, Belinda?' He smiled. 'You've got youth on your side, remember.'

Belinda grunted. 'Says who?'

'Take no notice,' Tracy advised Mike. 'She loves it really!'

'No, I don't.' Belinda slumped over her handlebars and took deep breaths.

'Count your blessings,' Mike said. 'I've just been on safari in Kenya with a bunch of adults. Some of them were well over forty, and they didn't take to the heat too well, I can tell you.'

'But can we have a breather?' Belinda gasped, unimpressed.

'OK, go ahead. True, they didn't have to cycle

up mountains,' he went on. 'We just took a look at the big game reserves, then travelled back up river by boat. All nice and civilised.'

'Wow!' Tracy sounded envious. 'How did you get a job like that? I guess you get to go all round the world!'

'I get about,' Mike said modestly. 'I worked for a spell last year in South America. And after Butterpike Hall, I plan to move on to Canada.'

'Sounds like a great life,' Tracy said. She loved the sound of exotic places and stiff physical challenges.

'Tell me that again at the end of the week,' Mike laughed. 'It's much more likely that you'll be begging to sit in front of a TV with your feet up for the rest of your lives!'

'No way!' Tracy protested and mounted her bike, ready for the ride down Butterpike Fell.

'Exactly right!' Belinda agreed with him. 'But you have to understand, there's no time to do important things like watch TV with these two around!' She pointed to Holly and Tracy, groaning as she sat back on her hard saddle and pointed the bike downhill.

'How come?' Mike rode alongside, taking the ridges and rocky bumps with perfect balance.

'We're in a kind of club,' she explained. 'All three

15

of us are mystery-mad, so we set it up to read books and talk about them, and that led us one way and another to solving real life mysteries.'

'Really?' He sounded amused. 'Regular Sherlock Holmeses, eh?'

Belinda's bike hit a rock. She bounced and wobbled. 'You'd be amazed,' she told him. She launched into a description of crimes solved by the Mystery Club. Mike stared with interest at Holly and Tracy as they made their way skilfully downhill.

'Belinda seems to have hit it off with Mike,' Holly observed as she glanced behind.

'I think she's trying to get on his good side so he'll give her an easy challenge!' Tracy joked.

As they chatted, they arrived at a spot where the drovers' track had to cross a narrow tarmac road. They pulled up to let a blue car pass by. It had slowed down for a cattle grid. Suddenly Tracy and Holly saw the back door fly open and a passenger roll out sideways on to the grass verge.

'Watch out!' Holly yelled at Belinda, who had come up from behind. A boy of about their own age scrambled to his feet as the car skidded to a halt.

'Wow!' Tracy watched as the boy sprinted uphill. He headed towards them, running blindly away from the car. Two men jumped out, slammed their doors shut and shouted as they began to give chase.

'What should we do?' Belinda demanded.

'We can't just stand here!' Holly decided in a flash. Without knowing what was going on, she turned her bike and prepared to ride off-road, across the rocky slope after the boy.

'Stop him!' one of the men shouted. 'Don't let him get away!' But the boy was fit. He was gaining ground.

'Why? What's he done?' Tracy waited a couple of seconds until the men ran by.

'He's on the run,' the other man stopped to explain. His grey suit and black leather shoes hampered his running action. He was bald and slightly overweight. 'We were taking him to a detention centre in Kendal, but he's gone and given us the slip!' He ran on again, but they could see how much ground he'd already lost.

The boy could certainly move. He cut diagonally across a slope of loose, flat grey stones, sending them sliding and crashing as he scrambled out of view. Soon he was hidden behind a tower of tall black rocks.

By now Mike Sandford had joined Tracy. 'Careful, Holly! He's on the run!' Tracy shouted.

Holly heard, nodded and kept going. She abandoned her bike to follow the runaway over the scree slope. The least she could do was to keep him in sight. She felt her footing slide dangerously, and decided to grab on to low bushes anchored by their roots into the thin soil. She could hear one of the men clambering noisily after her. By now, the boy was well out of sight.

Mike took in the scene at a glance. 'You stay here,' he told Tracy, Belinda and the rest of the group. 'Just in case it turns nasty.' He set off on foot, making good progress at first over the stretch of rough heather.

Belinda stared at Tracy. Holly was well ahead of the three men, about to vanish out of sight. 'You heard what Mike said,' she reminded her.

They thought of Holly up there, hot on the heels of a fugitive. 'Let's go!' Tracy declared. 'Like she said, no way can we just stand here!'

'He told us to stay put – you don't want to get into trouble on your first day,' urged Steffie. But Tracy and Belinda had already set off, sprinting for the slabs of black rock where the boy and Holly had disappeared.

Behind the tower of rocks, Holly came to a standstill. She could hear Mike's footsteps gaining on

18

her. She turned, glad that help was at hand. But she still couldn't see the boy. 'Where's he gone? He can't just have vanished into thin air!' she exclaimed. The landscape grew rockier, if anything steeper. But the dark, fleeing figure was nowhere to be seen.

Mike scanned the slope. A single sheep scuttled across the scree, setting off a landslide of small stones.

'Any sign?' One of the men from the car caught them up. He had longish fair hair and round glasses, dressed for the chase in jeans and trainers.

Mike clenched his jaw and stared ahead. 'Nope.' The empty hillside seemed to mock them. A large, grey bird rose from a shrub and wheeled in the air.

'What did he do?' Holly asked. She felt her breath come hard as she advanced with the men across the scree. Over the next ridge, she saw that the land fell away in an almost sheer slope, and at the foot of the slope lay the cool, clear water of the lake. No one could have escaped down that way.

'Theft, and now escaping from custody,' the older man told her. 'You wouldn't want to know him, believe me!'

Holly recalled her glimpse of the boy as he

bundled himself out of the car. He was slim and dark-haired, agile as he rolled on to the grass and leapt straight to his feet. She'd caught sight of his face and seen dark eyes scrunched up under frowning brows. He'd looked desperate. Now he'd disappeared and left them all guessing.

Mike turned at the sound of Tracy and Belinda's footsteps. 'I thought I told you to stay where you were!' His voice was edged with annoyance. He gathered the three girls together. 'Now look; you three stay right here. It's an order. You don't know the area; it's too dangerous for you to follow.'

They nodded sheepishly.

'Good. Come on, I'm with you now,' he told the two men. 'My guess is that he's headed for that next group of rocks up there, where there's plenty of cover. He'd just have had time to reach it.'

'OK, let's go.' The younger, fair-haired man set off again towards the rocks silhouetted against the skyline. Tracy, Holly and Belinda stood by, helpless onlookers.

Then, just as Mike reached the rocks, a figure sprang out and began to climb the sheer rock face.

'There!' Tracy yelled. She pointed. The men changed tack and began to climb after him. 'I

20

think they're gaining on him!' she said to Holly and Belinda. 'They should get him before too long.'

'Three against one,' Holly said quietly. The boy's face stuck in her mind.

Tracy scanned the horizon and pointed again. 'Look!' The boy had hauled himself up the rock face and stood on a ledge, pressed back, staring down at the water.

'He's going to jump!' Belinda gasped.

But the boy pivoted on the ledge and began to climb again.

'He must be desperate,' Holly said. Her stomach tightened into a knot at having to stand there watching.

'He'll break his neck if he's not careful,' Belinda said. The boy had made a reckless leap across a deep gap in the rocks as the men closed in on him from below.

Then there was a shout. The boy dropped out of sight, followed by the three men. They heard a slide and crunch of loose stones, more cries, the sounds of a scuffle. They caught a glimpse of blue against the dark rock; the boy's shirt, his face, then nothing. Loose stones cracked and rattled against the rock as they slipped over the edge into empty space.

21

Belinda grasped Tracy's arm. Her face was tight with fear. 'Someone's going to fall!' she gasped. 'I know it!'

'Shh!' Tracy whispered. They stood in silent dread. For a second, all went quiet and still.

'There must be something we can do!' Holly broke away from the others and headed for the rocks, in spite of Mike's orders. She hurtled towards the sounds of shouts and cries, which had begun again.

It took only a second for Belinda and Tracy to make the same snap decision. If help was needed, the three of them could give it together.

Then a loud cry rang out that stopped them dead. They looked up. The sun edged the rocky summit, the hillside was in shadow. But they heard that cry, and another sickening slide of loose stones, and they saw a shape plummet down.

Something fell from the rock face. A grey shape, spread-eagled in mid-air, its arms flung wide, falling, falling. There was silence.

Holly felt her heart lurch. She followed the descent of the shape which appeared to fall in slow motion. There was a splash. Circles rippled and widened across the smooth surface of the lake. She felt her heart click back into its rapid beat, sat heavily on the ground and held her head in her hands.

The body had sunk without trace.

3 An underwater search

'Oh, no!' Belinda was the first to find her voice after the fall.

'He dropped clean into the lake,' Tracy said quietly. They stood looking at one another, a hollow feeling of shock linking them together, horrified looks in their eyes.

'Did you see who it was?' Holly whispered.

Tracy shook her head. 'It happened too fast. Everything was a blur.'

Belinda turned to the other members of their group who had gathered on the road by the blue car. 'Get help!' she yelled. 'As fast as you can! Get the police. Get an ambulance!'

They watched as Ollie Swain broke away and cut down through the woods towards the Hall. Steffie and Mark Wright stood staring up at them, waiting for news.

'Maybe we won't need an ambulance,' Tracy said quietly, her voice flat and empty. She peered down into the water, but as yet there was no sign of anyone struggling to reach the surface. The lake seemed to have swallowed the body and wasn't ready to give it back up.

'Mike's OK, at any rate. Look!' Holly pointed with relief as their leader emerged from the shadow of the rocks. His shirt was torn across the sleeve, and his bare legs were grazed and cut. But he ran towards them, ordering them back.

'There's nothing we can do!' he gasped. His breath rasped in his throat. He looked wildly behind him.

'Who was it? Who fell?' Holly demanded. She saw another man stagger clear of the high rocks, minus his suit jacket, his shirt hanging open. 'It was the boy, wasn't it?' She turned to Mike, dreading the answer.

He nodded. His chest heaved, and he leaned against Tracy for support.

Holly bit her lip. Whatever he'd done, the runaway hadn't deserved to pay for it with his life.

'Let's go down,' Mike insisted. 'The other guy is trying to climb down to the water to see what he can do there, but I don't think there's much hope. That water is icy cold and it's deep.'

'We sent for the police and ambulance,' Belinda

told him. But the seconds ticked by, and she knew Mike was right; the longer the boy stayed under the water, the less chance there was of finding him alive.

But Tracy wasn't about to let someone drown while they sat around waiting for an ambulance to arrive. She broke free of Mike and began to sprint across the scree towards the water. Holly could see that she planned to skirt to one side of the sheer cliff face and arrive at the shore several metres up from where the fall had happened.

'What the—?' Mike spun round. He tried to make a grab for Holly as she too set off.

'Tracy's a good swimmer!' Holly yelled. 'She'll dive down to take a look. Come on!'

Mike and the car driver looked stunned as Belinda followed Holly and Tracy to the water's edge.

Tracy was the first to make it to the shore. She scrambled on to a flat rock overhanging the water's edge. She kicked off her shoes, and flung herself headlong into the lake.

Holly and Belinda held back. They hardly dared to look. There was a splash into the crystal clear surface, then they made out their friend's pale shape swimming underwater, down into the depths, kicking strongly.

At last Tracy's fair head broke the surface. She gasped in a great lungful of air. 'Nothing!' she yelled.

'Can you see down to the bottom?' Belinda cried. 'What's it like down there?'

'Clear, but deep. I'll try to go further this time. Hang on there!' Without delay, Tracy plunged down once more.

'It's too late. I'm sure it's too late,' Belinda whispered, shaking her head.

Holly glanced towards the road. A police siren wailed through the silence. She saw the car snake up the steep, narrow road, its blue light flashing. There was an ambulance in its wake. Figures ran out of the woods towards Mike Sandford, Ollie Swain at the head of them. He'd brought help from Butterpike Hall. Soon the spot would be crowded with onlookers.

'Come up, Tracy!' Holly urged, as she turned back to the lake. The water was still deadly calm. They saw Tracy's limbs, white under the surface, wavy and distorted. 'Thank heavens!' Holly cried, as she rose again to gulp in the air.

'Nothing!' Tracy reported, as soon as she could find her voice. She began to swim towards them.

'You're sure? Nothing at all?' Holly cried. She reached out to haul Tracy back on to the shore.

She imagined currents tugging at an unconscious body, pulling it down, pushing it far from the shore. 'No, don't go back in!' She held on to Tracy's arm. 'You're sure you didn't see anything?'

'Not a thing.' Reluctantly, Tracy let herself be pulled clear. She was shivering, and her teeth chattered. 'You can see for a long way, but even so, it's impossible to see the bottom. How deep *is* this lake?'

'Look!' Belinda peered far across the lake to where a police launch sped towards the spot. 'Best leave it to them now,' she said. She pointed to the paramedic team, and then to the police speedboat. 'They'll bring special equipment. They'll know what to do next.' She shook her head, as though she knew that it was too late in any case.

'Over here! Come quick!' Holly shouted. She wanted to cling on to her last shred of hope as the boat roared to a halt. It threw up spray on to the shore as it wheeled in the water and the engine cut out. She glanced sideways as the second man from the blue car ended his risky climb down the cliff face. He landed heavily on the stony shore. 'Did you see anything?' she asked.

He shook his head. 'No. I guess he fell clear of the rock at any rate. He just hit the water. He was probably knocked unconscious then. That would be it, I'm afraid!' He bent forward to rest his hands on his knees, drawing deep breaths. He ignored a bad cut across his forearm.

'You're bleeding!' Belinda went and offered him a handkerchief from her pocket to bind the wound. Meanwhile, Holly wrapped her sweat-shirt round Tracy's shoulders.

Suddenly, everything seemed to happen at once. A policeman in the launch began to shout instructions to the gathered onlookers. 'Stay back!' he ordered. The two paramedics scrambled along the shore, stretcher at the ready. Steffie, Mark and Ollie ran to the girls to check they were all OK. Mike and the car driver went to help bandage the third man's arm. Then a police frogman tipped backwards out of the boat. His wet suit smacked against the water before he vanished out of sight.

'Is everyone all right?' Jo Thomas, the leader from the centre, strode into the midst of things. She bent down to check that Tracy wasn't suffering any after-effects from her underwater search.

'I'm OK,' Tracy protested, shivering.

'Right, let's get you three back to the Hall,' Jo said firmly. 'Mike will stay to tell the police what they need to know.'

'Can't we wait and see what the diver finds?' Tracy pleaded.

Jo relented. 'OK, but I'm going to get the paramedics to check you over.' She saw that it would be cruel to take them away without firm news about the boy.

The two paramedics came and put a blanket round Tracy, took her pulse and gave her a glucose drink.

Holly closed her eyes, certain now that the boy had drowned. She stood next to Belinda, surrounded by activity. There was still no sign of the police diver, but she could overhear another police officer checking events with Mike and the two men from the blue car.

'Where were you taking him?' the policeman asked, his voice quiet and controlled.

'Kendal,' the older man replied.

'And could you give me your name, sir?'

'Tony Carter. I'm Daniel Martyn's careworker. He came into care after his arrest for theft, pending his trial. They'd just managed to find a place for him in a detention centre near Kendal. Rob Slingsby here is my assistant. That's where we were on our way to when all this happened.'

Holly heard the explanations given in a brisk tone. But now the boy had a name; Daniel.

'How old was the boy? Can you give a description?' the sergeant went on.

'Fifteen. I don't know much about him, though. His folks are abroad somewhere, apparently. He didn't give much away when he came into care. He was the sullen, silent type.'

'Appearance? Any distinguishing features for identification?'

'A bit unkempt. Dark, longish hair, thin face, brown eyes. I think he had a small mole on his left cheek, here. Tallish; about six foot. He gave the impression that he might work out in a gym. Not to be messed with; you know the sort.'

'OK, Mr Carter. That should do. Now tell me a bit about what happened when he fell.'

Holly opened her eyes to look at Belinda. 'This is my fault!' she gasped, still praying for a miracle, still wishing and hoping that the diver would surface with a body in his arms, unconscious but alive.

'No!' Belinda was quick to deny it.

'Yes! If I hadn't been so keen to chase after Daniel, he'd still be alive! He would have got away, running for cover before the social workers even realised he was gone.'

Belinda shook her head. 'If it's your fault, then it's *all* our faults,' she insisted. 'We all chased after him.'

'Hey, now!' Jo Thomas cut in. 'Let's keep a hold on things here, shall we?' She came and talked earnestly to the girls. 'This kid *chose* to run. He chose to escape from the car. He chose to climb that rock. *He* took the risk. If it didn't work out for him, that's not your problem!'

Holly's eyes filled with tears, but she nodded.

'OK!' Jo gave her a quick hug. 'Anyway, we still don't know for sure that he's not still alive.'

Mike stood close by. He turned and said quietly, 'Don't kid yourself. I don't see how anyone could survive this long underwater.'

Belinda swallowed a groan. 'Let's go,' she said. 'I can't take much more of this.'

'No, wait! Here's the diver now!' Holly cried.

The rubber hood and mask of the swimmer came into view. He took out the mouthpiece connected to his airhose and signalled to the boat. 'Negative!' he shouted. 'Not a thing! I'd say it looks pretty hopeless!'

Jo heard. Her grey-green eyes searched deep into Holly's. 'That's it, I'm afraid,' she said gently.

Holly shook her head.

'Holly, we can't do any more. Let's go,' Belinda insisted.

Even Tracy stood up. 'I guess we should,' she said.

So Holly walked away. She felt Jo's arm round her shoulder, but everything was a daze. A boy she

32

hadn't known had fallen to his death. He'd toppled through the air, arms flung wide. He'd hit the water and vanished. He would never come up alive. And try as she might to believe otherwise, she walked back to the Hall in the absolute certainty that she had played a part in his death.

That night, in the girls' dormitory at Butterpike Hall, many unanswered questions still hung in the air.

'Why did he take such a risk?' Holly whispered to Belinda and Tracy, lying in the beds next to hers. 'Even rolling out of the car when it was still moving was a gamble!'

'Let alone climbing that sheer rock face,' Belinda agreed.

'He must have had an awful lot to run away from,' Tracy whispered.

Holly nodded. 'He was desperate all right.'

'Who knows? Maybe he was innocent.' The idea struck Belinda for the first time. 'I know we only got a glimpse of him as he ran past, but he didn't look like you'd expect a kid like that to look.' She couldn't put it into words, but she felt uneasy about branding him guilty.

'I guess we'll never know,' Tracy whispered.

'This isn't the kind of mystery I like!' Holly

protested. Jo had told them earlier that the police search, which had gone on after they left, had turned up nothing. 'In one way it would have been better if they'd found a corpse. At least a body would be a certainty.' She pulled the cool white sheets high under her chin.

'Oh dear,' Belinda sighed. 'Mike says this is one of the deepest lakes in the country. It's a sheer drop underwater for hundreds of metres, with cross-currents that drag objects that fall into the water down to the bottom. What chance was there of finding anything down there, when you think about it?'

They fell silent as Jo Thomas came into the room for a last word with them before bedtime. She stood by the end of Tracy's bed. 'I wanted to say a couple of things before we put this episode behind us,' she began.

Propped on her elbows, Holly listened to Jo's calm voice.

'First of all, well done,' she said.

'How come?' Tracy shook her head.

'For raising the alarm. For doing the best you could.' She smiled at Tracy. 'I hear you're quite a swimmer!' She paused. 'You all did what you thought was right; I know that.'

'But?' Belinda guessed there was more to come.

'But Mike tells me you went against his orders, not just once, but a couple of times.' Jo didn't sound severe; more disappointed in them. 'That's important when you come here to Butterpike. If people don't follow orders, all kinds of things can go wrong. Our leaders are very experienced. You have to trust them; otherwise we all end up in a mess.'

There was nothing they could say, except sorry. Each one sounded ashamed as they had to admit they'd been in the wrong.

Jo rounded things off. 'Well, that's the end of my "talk" But it's not the end of the world. Like I said, you acted for the best and you did everything you could humanly do. Now there's just one more thing,' she added gently.

Holly hugged her knees to her chest. She glanced at Tracy and Belinda, who seemed as miserable as she felt herself.

'You three have had a shock today, and it occurs to me that you might not want to go on with the course.' She put a question into her tone of voice, looking at them each in turn.

For a second there was silence. Holly met Belinda's gaze. 'Oh, no!' Belinda said. 'We want to stay. I mean, *I* want to stay. I wouldn't want to go home. It'd be sort of giving in, wouldn't it?'

'Sure?' Jo smiled and checked with the other two.

'Sure!' Tracy agreed.

Holly nodded too. 'Belinda's right. She's changed her tune since we first arrived, but I agree. We want to see this through!' She smiled at Belinda.

'OK.' Jo stood up. 'I think that's a good decision. Now, let's try and put all this behind us, shall we?' She turned, ready to go. 'We meet at nine-thirty tomorrow morning in the games room, OK?'

They nodded.

'So get a good night's sleep.' She smiled as she headed for the door. 'You'll need it, believe me!'

4 Solving clues

'I take it you've all seen a compass before?' Mike Sandford began briskly. He'd gathered his group together in the games room and held up a clear plastic disc attached to a thick red cord. 'And you've all seen an Ordnance Survey map?' He grinned, as if he knew today's challenge would be a good one. 'It has these squares drawn on it. They're grid references which you use to plan a route. OK so far?' he asked.

Holly, Tracy and Belinda found they had to concentrate. They had to follow Jo's advice, put all thoughts of the previous day aside and listen hard.

'First you have to find your way up these three peaks.' He pointed the the thin, whirling, brown contour lines to the north of the lake. 'Following the grid references I give you and using your compasses, I want you to make your way back to Butterpike Hall by six this evening.'

'What do we do then?' Tracy made it sound like a piece of cake; just climbing three mountains in one day!

Belinda groaned.

'Then . . .' Mike looked as if he was enjoying himself. 'After you've eaten, you collect your torches, your emergency whistles and your bivvy bags, and you set off again!'

'Bivvy bags?' Belinda stared at the large orange plastic bag which Mike held up on display.

'For a bivouac on top of this peak here.' He pointed to a spot on the map beyond Butterpike Fell. 'It's pretty cold up there at night, even at this time of year. You need your bivvy bags to sleep in, your head-torches, and your maps and compasses, of course.'

'You mean, we get to sleep out?' Tracy suddenly came alive.

Mike nodded. 'That's the general idea. By daybreak, you have to be heading on this track down the fellside, aiming to arrive back at the Hall for breakfast at eight.'

'We'll freeze to death!' Belinda muttered, casting a feeble look in Holly's direction. 'Will someone please explain why I told Jo I wanted to stay?'

Holly grinned and took a deep breath. It certainly

38

seemed a difficult challenge. She just hoped they were up to it.

'Now, to make sure you all follow the full route, I drop in some clues which you have to solve. They're written down here, with grid references for you to find. And you mustn't come back without solving all the clues. That way I can check you've followed the correct route.' Mike turned to Belinda. 'This bit should suit you three mystery fans down to the ground.'

Steffie grinned. 'Big mouth!' she teased.

'So, for instance, in the daytime training exercise, I might pick up a grid reference and drop in a clue: say, "F7: How many steps up to the door of the dog's home?" And you can only solve that clue by going the correct way.'

'I get it!' Tracy pointed to the map. 'The dog's home. That's Rover's Cottage, isn't it?'

Mike raised his eyebrows and smiled. 'Could be,' he said. 'You'll have a number of clues like that. And remember, I'll be out there checking up on you!'

'Hey, this sounds great! Come on, you two!' Tracy was already heading for the door. She was dressed in shorts and sweat-shirt, with a pair of good walking boots and a small rucksack for drinks, food and emergency first aid. She'd grabbed a map in its plastic wallet and hung it round her neck. 'Pass me a compass while you're there, Holly!'

Holly joined her. 'Ready, Belinda?'

'As ready as I'll ever be.' Belinda grimaced at Mike. 'No, hang on a second! I forgot that extra pack of biscuits I've got stashed away upstairs in my locker!' She dashed off to fetch them, flew downstairs again and stuffed the biscuits down the front of her rucksack. 'You never know when we might be glad of these extra rations,' she pointed out.

Mike laughed. 'We're not sending you out into the Siberian desert, you know!'

'Practically!' Belinda longed to spend the night in her own cosy bed in the dormitory.

He tutted, watching good-humouredly as Belinda slung her rucksack across her shoulders. 'And remember, it's good for you!' He stood at the door and waved them off.

Belinda trudged off after Holly and Tracy. 'Good luck!' Jo Thomas called out from her office down the corridor.

Outside, the weather was misty, but the forecast was good. By the time Holly, Tracy and Belinda had got their bearings and trekked halfway up the first of the three peaks, the mist had cleared, and they had to solve the first of Mike's clues.

'OK,' Tracy said. She spread her map on a flat rock and looked round for landmarks. 'We've reached the grid reference for the first clue. I guess we're still a couple of kilometres short of Rover's Cottage, which is clue number three. Our first one says, "The high road or the low road. Which is the quickest way to quench my thirst?"' She looked up at Holly and Belinda with a puzzled frown.

'I suppose that means we have to spot the quickest route to the nearest supply of fresh water,' Belinda suggested. 'But how?'

Holly gazed all round. To their left, about fifty metres up a track, was a wooden signpost, with arms pointing in three different directions. 'I bet that'll give us the answer!' She pointed to it and jogged up to the post. 'This way points to Skiddaw!' she shouted. 'This one says to High Force; five kilometres. And this low track goes to High Force as well, but it's five and a half kilometres!'

Belinda and Tracy studied the map. 'Skiddaw is that mountain there.' Tracy found the name printed way to the north of their grid reference. 'Now, High Force; what could that be?' she asked, looking round for a clue.

Belinda continued to pore over the map. 'Here it is!' she exclaimed. 'High Force. It's printed along a blue line that shows a stream. It's where the

41

contour lines all squash together. I wouldn't be surprised if High Force is a waterfall!'

'And the high road is the quickest way from here,' Holly said as she joined them. 'Let's write it down.' She took out a pen to jot down the answer to the first clue. 'The low road is half a kilometre longer, so we have to say the high road. There!'

Satisfied, Tracy folded her map. 'Now for the second clue!' she said. She began to stride ahead.

'Is there no stopping that girl?' Belinda moaned, stopping to nibble at a chocolate biscuit which she'd taken out of her rucksack. She offered one to Holly.

'No. You should have realised that by now,' Holly laughed and took a biscuit. 'Good for our energy level. Thanks!'

'In that case, I won't offer one to Tracy,' Belinda sighed. 'She doesn't need one!'

Grumbling and teasing, they followed after their athletic friend.

The day's climb, with its steep slopes, and its changes in terrain from rocky cliffs to deep woodland and meandering rivers, had whipped up their appetites again by the time they returned to the Hall. It was five o'clock. They'd snacked on crisps, fruit, and Belinda's favourite chocolate biscuits, but now they were glad to tuck straight into an enormous pile of new potatoes, cheese pie and peas.

'We need to stock up for tonight,' Belinda said, helping herself to salad. The cafeteria was already buzzing with other kids back from orienteering and windsurfing. Knives and forks clattered, steam rose from the serving hatches as people jostled and queued for food.

'It sounds to me like you're secretly looking forward to it,' Holly said. She nudged Tracy's elbow.

'No way,' Belinda protested.

'Well, I am!' Tracy insisted. She fiddled with the head-torch which Mike had issued to each of them. It strapped round the forehead and shone ahead like a miner's lamp. 'Orienteering in the dark. It sounds really wild!'

The only drawback, when they set off up the fellside later that evening, was that the route took them close to the scene of yesterday's fall. All three were silent as they passed by the spot, which was gloomier than ever in the gathering dusk. No one dared to cast a glance sideways down into the dark water. Holly shivered at the memory, but pressed on up the hill. She fixed her attention on the map and looked straight ahead.

'Not so fast,' Belinda said. 'I can't keep up this pace!' Darkness was falling, so she switched on her torch.

'The sooner we reach the summit, the sooner we can snuggle down into our bivvy bags and have a good sleep,' Holly told her. She held her compass flat in the palm of her hand and studied it carefully.

'How do you snuggle into an orange plastic bag?' Belinda pointed out. 'OK, OK, I'll keep quiet!' she promised, as Holly gave her a fixed stare.

Tracy strode ahead into the darkness. 'We're making pretty good time. What's the next grid reference, Holly?'

'F7.' By now it was so dark, she had to shine the beam of her torch directly at the map and set of instructions. 'We have to follow the track well to the east of Rover's Cottage, the place we saw earlier. You know, the third clue we had to solve.' Rover's Cottage had turned out to be a disused shepherd's hut, its stone roof already crumbling and falling in. 'Then we head up the pass over Butterpike Fell, see?'

Tracy bent her head to look. 'Yes, got that. The cottage must be the last sign of civilisation up here. From now on, it's going to be pretty deserted.' She went on ahead, eager to meet the next stage of the challenge. Their narrow track snaked across a scree slope, forcing them to go in single file, looking straight ahead.

It was the most difficult part of the walk so far. Holly kept the beam of her head-torch fixed firmly on the ground a metre or so in front of her, unable to look either to left or right. The path demanded her full attention. She covered a kilometre or so without looking up. The only sound was the crunch of her boots on the track. A pale new moon shone overhead, and to either side the mountains loomed.

At last she joined Tracy on a small plateau where they could pause and rest.

'Isn't this great?' Tracy breathed. 'Sleeping on a mountaintop with no one around!'

'Oh, so they're mountains now, are they?' Holly laughed. She hitched her rucksack into a more comfortable position, then turned to look down the slope for Belinda's torch-beam following them up. 'Hey, Belinda, Tracy admits it's a mountain we're climbing!' Her voice echoed down the empty hillside. 'Where is she? Where's Belinda?'

Tracy frowned. Her torch-beam raked across the track they'd just climbed, but no figure toiled up it. 'It was pretty hard going down there,' she reminded Holly. 'I guess we'd better hang on here and wait for her.'

'Maybe the battery in her torch failed,' Holly suggested. She tried to make out a moving shape amongst the rocks and boulders. But the darkness was thick and black. It was impossible to pick out Belinda's progress.

'When did you last notice she was behind you?' Tracy's voice turned serious. Minutes were ticking by, and there was still no sign of Belinda.

'Back down by the derelict cottage. I remember she was moaning on about having to sleep in a bivvy bag, then she promised to keep quiet.' Holly felt a wind begin to whistle through her hair. She zipped up her fleece jacket. 'Tracy,' she said, 'you don't think Belinda could have . . .?'

'Got lost?' Tracy jumped in as Holly hesitated. 'Oh, no way!' She tried to sound confident. 'She has a map, just like us, doesn't she? No, she can't possibly be . . .'

'Lost.' Holly finished the sentence for Tracy. The silence drew in round them like a fog. 'But what if her torch did fail? How would she read her map?'

'She would have blown her warning whistle to make us stop,' Tracy said. It was hopeless trying to peer down the mountainside, but she tried anyway.

A cold feeling crept down Holly's spine. It would be so easy to fall on that narrow, steep stretch of track. She couldn't bear it if anything serious had happened to Belinda.

'Belinda!' she yelled, at the top of her voice. Echoes bounced back, but no reply floated up through the darkness.

'Belinda!' Tracy joined in, using her whistle, too. Then: 'It's no good, we'll have to go back and look for her,' Tracy decided.

Holly nodded. 'She's lost all right.' She pictured Belinda losing her footing on the narrow track, slipping, sliding in the dark, perhaps knocking her head, or breaking a limb. Quickly they turned, half-running, half-scrambling back the way they'd come.

'You know what a terrible head for heights she has!' Tracy gasped.

'You don't think she's fallen?' Holly voiced her fears. Now, in her mind's eye, she saw a crumpled shape lying at the bottom of a sheer drop, or hurtling down a rough, stony slope until it slumped to a halt in the valley bottom.

'No!' This time Tracy didn't sound so confident. She jumped and leapt down the slope as fast as she could.

'Belinda!' Holly cried. 'Where are you?'

There was no answer.

5 Rover's Cottage

Belinda woke up with a start. How long had she
been asleep, she wondered. It was one thing to give
way to the temptation to take a snack and a short
rest while Holly and Tracy forged ahead. After all,
three peaks in one day was enough to tire anyone
out, let alone this mad attempt to climb a mountain
in the dark. So she'd taken off her rucksack and
sat down against a rock, planning a five minute
breather so that she could eat a biscuit, regain
her energy and catch up with the others. She'd
shone her head-torch into her rucksack, taken
out one of her favourite sort wrapped in gold
foil, eaten it, then rested her head against the
heather.

But it was another thing to actually fall asleep.
Now she'd lost sight of Holly and Tracy, and
she found that the battery in her head-torch was
already beginning to fade. That must mean she'd
been asleep for some time. She rubbed her eyes

and looked at her watch in the dim yellow light. It was ten minutes past midnight.

'Oh, no, I'll never live this down!' she muttered. She picked up her rucksack and slung it over one shoulder. Pride made her decide not to call or whistle for help. She would try to reach the top of the mountain by herself, with the aid of her fading torch.

She decided to read the map and memorise her route, then head for the bivvy point. 'Come on, Belinda Hayes,' she told herself firmly, 'this is when you prove what you're made of!'

She studied the map for a minute or two. *Simple*, she thought. *There's really only one path I can follow, except for sheep tracks, and they won't count*. It was just a case of following her nose until she arrived. She folded the map and returned it to its envelope, then braced herself for the effort ahead.

Uphill all the way, she reminded herself. *What can possibly go wrong?*

She glanced at the moon; not much light would come from that slim little silver shape tonight, and clouds scudded across the sky, blocking out the stars. Should she conserve the battery in her torch and switch it off? Or should she rely on its faint beam for as long as it lasted? She wished to goodness that she hadn't left it switched on as she'd drifted into sleep. Unnerved by the pitch dark when she tried to walk without the torch, she decided to leave it on. She felt her heart sink as it grew fainter and fainter. Still, she was determined to catch up without making a fuss. Her mouth was dry, the palms of her hands sticky as she pressed ahead.

'Belinda!' Holly yelled from way up the mountain-side. Her voice drifted into the vast empty space.

'Holly, over here!' Tracy heard a noise in the undergrowth. 'There's something behind this rock!' She scrambled towards it, desperately hoping that she wouldn't find Belinda injured and only half-conscious after a nasty fall from the steep track.

'Is it her?' Holly's heart was in her mouth as she followed Tracy down.

'I can't see. Did you hear anything? I'm sure I did!' They set up a frantic search, beating and kicking at the bushes with their arms and feet.

'Belinda?' Holly pulled back and went more cautiously. She heard another scrambling sound, a faint bleat.

'Oh!' Tracy cried out in surprise as a ewe and her lamb rose from the heather. They lurched down the slope, bleating in annoyance at being disturbed. Tracy fell backwards into some bushes, and Holly leapt on to the rock out of harm's way. The sheep and lamb blundered off, and with fast beating hearts, Tracy and Holly continued the search.

Strange, Belinda thought, as she squinted at her compass, *I thought I was heading north-east. Maybe I'm not so good at this orienteering lark after all!* The reading on the disc said north-west. She adjusted her direction and took a much narrower track. Woody branches of heather scratched at her legs and tugged her back. Her torchlight was only a weak yellow glow.

I'm sure I've seen that pointed rock before! she said to herself. The track dipped into a deep hollow. But she decided that one rock looked pretty much the same as another in the dead of night. She pressed on regardless, trying to read her compass and make out landmarks on the horizon. She pictured arriving triumphant on the summit. Even an orange bivvy bag seemed like the lap of luxury to her now, as she stumbled on through the rough heather.

'Uh-oh!' Surprise made her speak out loud. Her boot had kicked against a solid wooden object, half hidden by the low bushes. She bent to push them aside. It was what she feared; a sign at ground level, with an arrow pointing to the left. It had peeling, faded letters in black paint. She read them with a sinking heart. 'Rover's Cottage'. She was just able to make it out before her weak torch-beam packed in altogether. 'Oh, no! I've gone round in one great big circle!' she groaned.

She sat heavily on the ground to contemplate what to do next. By now Holly and Tracy would be way ahead. They would suppose that Belinda just hadn't been fit enough to make it, that at some point she'd quietly given in and gone back to the Hall, rather than give them any problem to deal with because of her tiredness. Anyway, her legs ached. No way could she now think of making it to the top.

She sighed and looked round. As her eyes gradually got used to the near total darkness, she thought she could make out the shape of the tumbledown cottage at the end of the path. She decided that this would be the best shelter she could find; a place to rest until morning. She kicked her tired legs into action and made her way down the overgrown path.

Rover's Cottage nestled in a hollow, out of the worst wind and weather. Even so, it was dilapidated now, and looked as if it hadn't been lived in for years. Belinda stretched out her hand to feel the moss-covered surface of the stone. She tried the door handle. It was locked. But inside she could hear a dry, scraping noise, as if her attempt to open the door had disturbed something.

She shivered and glanced round. Should she press on, or retreat on to the vast, dark moorland? Gathering her courage, she decided to try to find a way into the cottage, through a window perhaps. Anything was better than the chilly feeling that had just crept into her bones.

Sure enough, the glass in the window to the left of the door was missing. There was no bolt, and it was low enough for her to sit on the stone sill and ease her legs into the room. Belinda gave a little jump and landed on bare floorboards. 'Great!' she sighed. She would take a quick look round to see if she could find what had made that strange noise; an animal seeking shelter, a trapped bird? Then she would find the driest, cleanest corner for herself and climb inside her bivvy bag. She would sleep out the night.

Holly and Tracy fell silent as they continued their search. Worry held them tight in its grip. They'd come a long way back down Butterpike Fell, and still there was no sign of Belinda.

'Holly, I think this could be serious!' Tracy whispered, almost afraid to break the silence. 'Surely we should have seen some sign of her by now!'

'Shh!' Holly signalled. She stooped to pick something off the track. It glittered beside a large boulder, caught in her torchlight; a piece of gold wrapping from one of Belinda's favourite chocolate bicuits. She showed it to Tracy. 'What do you think; coincidence?' she asked.

Tracy considered it with knitted brows. 'No, I think it means we're on the right track at last.'

'Me too.' Holly's hopes revived as she pocketed the wrapper. 'I wonder what's wrong, though. She wouldn't usually be so careless.' With a worried frown, she carried on down the hill.

Belinda poked her way across the empty room, then opened a door on to a narrow hallway. The place smelt damp and disused, but she thought she detected a lingering smell of wood smoke coming through the closed door opposite. *That's odd*, she thought, *to smell smoke in a place that hasn't been lived in for years!* She pushed the door. It creaked as it slowly swung open.

There was a candle alight in a bottle on the table and embers of a wood fire in the old grate. A tap dripped. There were cans of Coke lying empty on the wooden draining-board. In the glow of the fire, Belinda could make out an old iron cooking-range inside a stone arch, a bare table with a chair tipped forward against it. One of the Coke cans rocked, then rolled to the floor, as if someone had just disturbed it. And whoever it was must have been in a great hurry.

Belinda drew a sharp breath. She grasped the edge of the door, surprised to see that her planned night's shelter was already occupied. But by whom? This was someone's temporary home; that much was plain. She decided the best thing was to leave. She began to back out across the hallway.

But just as Belinda reached the door, the handle began to turn slowly from the outside. Someone pushed and rattled the lock. Belinda froze. She felt trapped. Which way now? The house gave her the creeps, but she was forced back into the first, empty room, tiptoeing softly across the hollow floorboards. One creaked. She froze again.

Then something scratched at the outside of the window. *Scrabble, scrabble*. Belinda couldn't make it out. She backed against the wall, as a white blur appeared at the glass, and a hand tried to clear a patch in the dirt. Fingers squeaked against the pane.

Belinda screamed. The window flew open.

'Holly!' Belinda sank back against the wall. The blurred face at the window was her best friend, and soon Tracy followed her over the windowsill into the bare room. 'Tracy!' Belinda gasped. 'What are you two doing here?'

'You look like you saw a ghost,' Tracy said, hands on hips, wrinkling her nose at the damp, airless smell. Giant cobwebs caught in the beam of her torch. It scanned the rough plaster walls, piercing the gloom.

'We might well ask you the same question!' Holly retorted. 'We've spent ages trying to find you, thinking you'd fallen down some deep ravine and broken your leg!'

'At least,' Tracy said.

'Or worse.' Holly frowned.

'But no!'

'Here you are holed up in comfort for the night!'

'While the two of us went ahead, prepared to rough it on top of a mountain!' Tracy finished off.

'Just hold on a minute!' Belinda held up her hands. 'If you must know, I didn't do it on purpose. I stopped for a snack and I must have dozed off with my light on.' She gave it to them straight.

Holly and Tracy stared back open-mouthed.

'Yes, I know!' Belinda turned down her mouth at the corners. 'But it's easily done, believe me.

Then I decided to try and orienteer my way up to the top by myself, but I got lost, and my torch packed in altogether, then I stumbled across this old place!' Her explanation went full gallop, with Tracy and Holly too surprised to interrupt. 'I really am sorry!' she finished off.

It took a while for it all to sink in. Holly listened and looked at Belinda's embarrassed expression. 'You stopped for a snack?' she repeated. She turned to look at Tracy.

Tracy stared at Belinda. 'You dozed off?'

Belinda nodded and sighed. 'I said I was sorry.'

She looked so unhappy that the others burst into peals of laughter. Instead of telling her off for messing up the challenge, they saw the funny side.

'Oh, brilliant!' Tracy shouted. 'We were thinking up all kinds of disasters, and you were taking a nap! Typical!'

'Yes, but . . .' Belinda began.

'Well, never mind. We can still complete this course if we're quick.' Holly glanced at her watch. It was two-thirty. 'Not that we'll get much sleep once we've made it to the top and back to the Hall for eight o'clock, but that won't have to matter.' She grinned with relief. 'We're just glad you're safe!'

'But listen!' Belinda cocked her head to one side. 'I heard a sound inside the house before I came in, so I went through to the kitchen to take a look.' She beckoned them eagerly. 'What do you think of this?' she demanded, showing them the embers in the grate, the empty cans, a half-eaten packet of biscuits.

'Someone got here before us, that's for sure,' Tracy said with a shrug. 'So?'

'But who? And why would he or she take off as soon as I came near?' Belinda folded her arms. She felt safer in this creepy place now that Tracy and Holly had turned up. 'I mean, it's just weird!'

Holly advanced into the kitchen and began to poke round. She picked up the biscuit packet. 'Chocolate digestives,' she said and smiled at Belinda. 'One of your favourites!'

'Hey, look over here!' Tracy had made her way over to the sink to investigate the dripping tap. She aimed her head-torch at an enamel bowl half-full of water, and a strip of blue denim fabric soaking in it.

Belinda followed. 'Blood!' She put a hand to her mouth, as Tracy beckoned Holly to take a look. They all stared at the discoloured water in the bowl.

'Are you sure?' Gingerly Tracy put her fingertip

58

into the bowl and poked the cloth. 'Couldn't it be rust or something?'

'It looks more like blood,' Holly said. 'But whose?' She too dipped in the tips of her fingers. A rusty red cloud stirred and whirled in the white bowl.

'Whoever the denim stuff belonged to?' Tracy guessed. The strip of cloth was about thirty centimetres long and six centimetres wide.

'And that could be whoever decided to make a quick getaway when I first came in.' Belinda backed uneasily towards the door. 'Maybe he or she's hurt?'

'But not badly. Otherwise, how could he or she have run off?' Holly asked. She studied the flickering candle flame, dying out in the bottle. 'And whoever it was is probably pretty annoyed at the interruption.'

Tracy nodded. 'Let's go! We're not going to get any further with this right now. Let's think about it while we walk.' The sooner they were out of this place the better. She felt spooked by the blood in the bowl.

'But what about all this?' Holly asked. She was reluctant to leave things up in the air.

'Shh!' Belinda's ears strained for any unusual sound. She thought she heard stealthy footsteps through the heather outside; the gentle brushing against the bushes, the faint crunch of a footfall. 'Someone's coming. Come up here!' she hissed, bundling Holly and Tracy up the creaking stairs. 'Turn off those torches, keep your head down. I don't like the sound of this!' The mysterious occupant of Rover's Cottage was returning.

The Mystery Club crouched on the upstairs landing, waiting with bated breath.

This time, the intruder didn't bother with niceties. He tried the locked door. It stuck fast. He kicked at it with a heavy boot. Then he shoulder-charged it. They heard the wood splinter and the old rotten hinges give way. They huddled in an unseen corner as he flung aside the door and barged down the passage into the sitting-room on the left. Then he tried the kitchen on the right. They heard him scatter empty cans, they saw the candle flame flicker long shadows into the hallway and then die out. A torch-beam came on instead.

The intruder rushed out to the foot of the stairs.

'Stay down!' Belinda warned. They crouched lower in the dusty corner.

'I know you're up there, you little swine!' he yelled. 'Don't think you can get away this time!' The voice was a snarl, but there was a recognisable tone.

Holly sprang to the head of the stairs. 'Mike, it's us!' she yelled, taking the stairs two at a time. Tracy and Belinda flew down after her.

They came face to face with Mike Sandford.

'*You* three!' he said. His face registered shock. He pushed them aside and mounted the stairs, searching roughly through the two upstairs rooms, slamming doors as he went. When he came back down, he seemed calmer. 'Could someone tell me what on earth you're doing here?' he asked. 'Why aren't you bivvying up on the fell?' He took Holly by the elbow and led her back into the kitchen, then took a second to note the chaos.

Belinda cleared her throat. 'It's my fault. I got lost. The other two had to come looking for me.'

'Lost?' Mike repeated. 'How did you get split up from the others?'

Holly began to see how foolish they must look. 'It could happen to anyone,' she protested feebly.

'Oh, yes!' he said, eyebrows raised, a half-smile on his face.

'Anyhow, we plan to get right on and complete the course,' Tracy told him, eager to salvage their reputations. 'Is that OK?'

Mike waved a hand round the room. 'I'm not sure I believe any of this. It looks to me like you were planning a cosy little party for yourselves!'

'But!' Belinda cut in. 'But *we* didn't do this!'

'What do you mean?'

'This place was like this when I arrived.'

Mike seemed taken aback. Then a set expression slipped across his face. 'Yeah, yeah!' he teased. 'A likely story! It couldn't be that you're just trying to get yourselves off the hook, could it?'

'No!' Belinda reacted quickly. She might be a hopeless orienteer, but she was no liar.

'So how come you were so far off course? How come you were so slack in the first place?' He walked across the kitchen, then he turned to face them. 'Well, you can forget any idea you say you have about completing this particular challenge,' he said. 'It's too late for you to pick up where you left off.'

'Hang on!' Tracy stuck out her chin. 'Can't we have another chance? I still think we can finish the course by morning!'

'No way.' Mike strode off again. This time, his glance fell on the bloodstained rag in the bowl. A shock seemed to jolt through him like an electric current, but he said nothing. 'Just do as you're told,' he insisted. 'I have a job to do; Steffie, Mark and Ollie to check up on. They take their challenges seriously, unlike some other people

62

I might mention! I can't hang around here any longer!'

They backed off out of the kitchen towards the front door. It hung at an angle off one of its hinges.

'Now listen, you three. Get yourselves straight back to the centre. I'm saying it clearly, in words of one syllable. Go back to the Hall!' Mike stood blocking the kitchen doorway. 'And tomorrow morning, I plan to check up to see if that's what you did. No messing about, OK?' His deep voice brooked no argument.

Holly looked dejectedly at Tracy and Belinda. Mike didn't think they were up to the challenge, so they did as they were told and set off down the hill in a wretched mood. Even worse, Jo Thomas and all the others would soon get to hear about this. Holly felt sure that Mike would see to that.

They trailed down the hillside into the dark cover of the ancient oak woods. An owl hooted. Unseen creatures scuttled through the undergrowth. Holly, walking ahead in silence, began to work through a hunch. 'You know something?' she said. The light over the entrance to Butterpike Hall glowed through the trees.

'No, what?' Tracy was almost too miserable to reply.

'Maybe it wasn't us Mike was looking for in the cottage.' She halted under a low, rustling branch.

Belinda paused to consider it. 'Maybe you're right. There *was* something about the way he broke in, like he was expecting to come up against someone else.' She recalled his forced entry, his angry words.

'Like the person who lit the fire and left all the stuff lying around?' Tracy caught the thread. 'We still don't know who that was.'

'Exactly.' Holly tried to look on the bright side. 'Maybe this is just the mystery we need to liven us up!'

'We could sure do with something,' Tracy agreed. Tomorrow they would still have to face everyone and admit they'd failed the orienteering task.

'A mystery to solve, and our names to clear.' There was fresh enthusiasm in Holly's voice.

'If Mike will let us, that is.' Belinda was the first to trudge forward on to the open lawn, exhausted and depressed.

'Why, what do you mean?' Holly was already racing through the obvious possibilities; a tramp, a traveller, a trespasser who'd already made a nuisance of himself at the Hall. Some intruder with a vendetta against Mike himself?

64

'I mean, I think he's going to make things pretty tough for us from now on,' Belinda replied in a gloomy tone. 'In fact, I think he's going to make life absolutely miserable!'

6 An ordeal

Belinda was right; by next day the adventure holiday at Butterpike Hall had turned into a grim ordeal.

After a couple of hours of broken sleep, Holly, Belinda and Tracy went down to the cafeteria. Holly held her head high as she took her tray of cereal and orange juice to a corner table, keeping her fingers crossed that not too many people had heard about them messing up the orienteering challenge of the night before.

'It was brilliant!' Ollie Swain sat down at the next table and described the thrill of success. He breathed in deeply. 'There's nothing to beat it, surviving on your wits, all alone against the elements. Terrific!'

Steffie dug him in the ribs with her elbow. 'Shh!' she warned. 'No need to go on about it!' She smiled kindly at Holly, obviously aware of her embarrassment. This was almost worse than Ollie's boasting.

'Pass the milk, please, Belinda,' Holly muttered, hiding her blushing face behind her hair. But the cereal tasted like soggy cardboard. She found she couldn't meet Jo Thomas's direct gaze when she strolled up to their table.

'I hear you got lost,' she said bluntly. She stood with her hands in her shorts pockets, studying all three of them.

'*I* did. It was my fault,' Belinda claimed.

'Well,' Jo shrugged. 'Whatever. There's no need to take it to heart. You're here to have some fun as well, remember.' She perched on the edge of a chair and leaned her elbow on the table. 'Look, I realise this week hasn't gone well for you so far.'

'You can say that again,' Tracy sighed.

'But we're not halfway through yet. There's plenty of time for you to pick up from this low point. Most people do find the orienteering challenge the most difficult exercise, so you're not alone.'

Holly wished they would all stop being kind. She pushed her cereal bowl to one side and rested her chin in her hands.

'Why not see what today brings?' Jo suggested. 'I don't know exactly what Mike has lined up for your group. It could be windsurfing or white-water rafting. Maybe that will turn out to be more your thing.' She stood up easily from the table. 'Chin up!' she said as she left.

But the task Mike Sandford held in store had none of the fun of sailing or shooting rapids. He sent the others off on an exciting challenge, then turned to Holly, Tracy and Belinda. They stood waiting in the yard. The weather was dull and heavy, to match their mood. 'See that empty oil-drum?' Mike pointed to a tall metal container standing in one corner.

They nodded.

'Well, the object of this exercise is to toughen you up,' he explained. This morning his grin contained no humour as he strode over to the barrel. 'You don't need brains to carry out this task. No clues to solve, no decisions to make!'

Holly felt her eyes widen into a blank stare.

'What's this guy got against us?' Tracy whispered to Belinda. 'What did we do that was so bad?'

Belinda shook her head. 'I don't know. But I suspect we're not his favourite people right now.' She squared her shoulders, ready for the worst.

'I want the three of you to get this big drum round the lake without getting lost. Nice and easy!' He tilted the drum. 'You can roll it, you can carry it, you can invent ways to get it across streams and over rocks, just as long as you get it back here by four this afternoon. OK?' He waited for the message to sink in. 'Now, I think even you three can manage this one! Ready?'

'I thought Jo just said we were here to have fun!' Belinda mumbled to Holly and Tracy.

Mike caught her dismay, laughed and fell back into his old, teasing way. 'Fun comes later,' he promised. He turned to smile at Holly. 'Tell Belinda I'm not such an ogre as she seems to think. It's just that there aren't enough windsurfing boards to go round, so Steffie, Mark and Ollie got to go first. It'll be your turn soon, and they'll be trying the oil-barrel challenge.'

Holly nodded. 'That's fair enough.'

'As long as we all get to be miserable!' Belinda noted. 'That makes everything fine!'

Mike was grinning as he tilted the drum towards them. 'We're not about to give in again, are we?'

'No, we're not.' Tracy went forward first and stood ready to take the weight from him.

Holly and Belinda joined her, and, gritting their teeth, they took the heavy drum and tipped it on to its side. It crashed with a hollow sound on to the stone flags, then rolled away from them.

Mike put out a foot to stop it. 'See you later,' he said cheerfully. 'Watch out for us on the lake.

Look out for four yellow-and-green windsurfing sails!' And he went off, leaving them to cope with their dull exercise.

'Don't say anything!' Tracy warned. 'Let's just do it!'

'The sooner the better,' Holly agreed. They put their weight behind the drum and rolled it down the path to the water's edge.

'Like I said, he doesn't want to make life easy for us,' Belinda groaned. She fixed her glasses firmly on her nose and set to. 'But no way is Mike Sandford going to get things all his own way!'

'Hold on, let's think about this!' Holly called when they reached the lake. She wedged a piece of wood under the barrel. 'How are we going to get this thing right round without breaking our backs? It must be at least three kilometres.'

'Driftwood!' Tracy said. She pointed to two long branches washed up on the pebbly shore.

'Rope!' Belinda spotted a rowing boat moored by a piece of good, strong nylon cable. She ran to drag the boat clear of the water, then untied the rope. 'The boat belongs to the centre, see!' She pointed to the intials BH stamped in black on the seat inside the boat. 'Butterpike Hall.'

'So we strap the oil-drum to the branches to make a kind of stretcher to carry it with?' Holly saw that the idea would work. 'We'll take it in turns; one at the front, one at the back, and one taking a rest, on a rota system!'

Glad to be busy, they got to work, and soon had the huge metal drum tied fast to the handy branches. 'He said we could invent ways to carry it,' Belinda said. She took the weight at the front of the drum. 'So come on, let's show him!'

They tramped forward with their heavy weight along the foot of the cliff, then across a fast-flowing stream that brought clear rainwater down from the mountains. 'How about trying to solve the mystery of Rover's Cottage?' Tracy suggested. 'Anything to take our minds off other problems.'

'Mike wouldn't like it,' Belinda tut-tutted. 'But then he's not here, is he?' She grinned cheekily.

'No, he's having a good time windsurfing!' Holly grunted. She glanced towards the lake, then stopped dead in her tracks.

'Ouch!' Belinda tried to walk ahead with the front end of the barrel, nearly pulling her arms out of their sockets as Holly stopped short.

'Sorry, Belinda. But I've just thought; if we did get in Mike's way at the cottage last night and scared off the person he was really looking for, don't you think maybe this barrel challenge is his way of keeping us out of the picture until things die down?' She looked eagerly at Tracy and Belinda. 'I'm sure something fishy is going on. Just think about what we've discovered so far!'

'Like a list of clues?' Belinda asked. 'Well, the first one at the cottage was the fire still alight in the grate. I take it we're trying to work out who was in that old place, and what Mike Sandford had against him?'

'Sure.' Tracy offered to take over the front of the drum from Belinda. 'The fact that the fire was still lit tells us that this person had left the house very recently. There were logs piled by the grate. That means he planned to stay and make himself comfortable, before he was interrupted.'

'Supposing it *was* a he,' Holly put in.

'Let's suppose.' Tracy was striding ahead along the rocky shore. 'Now, clue number two. The food and drink. That's pretty obvious too.'

'Right. This "he" had obviously stocked up,' Belinda said. She half ran to keep up with Tracy. 'I counted five or six empty cans around the place, and another six-pack unopened by the sink.' She recalled the scene exactly, searching her memory for further clues. 'I've got an idea!' She pulled Tracy to a sudden halt.

'Go on!' Holly urged. She felt huge spots of rain begin to fall cold and wet on her bare arms. Before long there would be a downpour, just to add to the joys of the day's activity.

Belinda went on rapidly. 'He must've bought the Coke somewhere local, right? I mean, two six-packs are not that easy to carry. What we have to do is check the local shop to see who bought all that drink. We'll get a description and start from there!'

Holly nodded. Pieces of the jigsaw began to slot together. She felt sure that they would soon learn the identity of the mysterious squatter in the deserted cottage. 'Let's do that as soon as we get back. There's only one village shop. We shouldn't have too much trouble picking up a few extra clues there!'

Feeling more cheerful in spite of the rain, they jogged along the shore. 'But what about clue number three?' Belinda asked. 'How do we figure out the blood?'

They thought in silence for a while. 'Go to the nearest doctor to ask if anyone's been treated for a deep cut, stitches, a tetanus shot, stuff like that?' Tracy suggested.

'They wouldn't be able to tell us,' Holly said. 'It's confidential information.'

'OK, we'll ask round the village; see if anyone's noticed that kind of injury,' Belinda volunteered.

73

'Not that I think this "he" would make it so obvious. He wouldn't want to be spotted that easily.'

'Hmm.' Holly considered all the angles. 'What about the strip of fabric soaking in the bowl? Blue. Blue denim. A neat strip torn from the bottom of a shirt, maybe? It wasn't thick enough to have come from jeans.'

Tracy and Belinda nodded. Their trainers squelched through puddles as the rain poured down. They were soaked to the skin. A sudden thought jolted Holly to a standstill.

'Wait a minute!' she cried. 'What colour shirt was Daniel wearing that day?' Rain streamed through her hair and down her face.

'Blue!' Tracy and Belinda said in the same split second. They dropped the barrel dead on the ground and stood staring at one another in the pouring rain. They pictured again a flash of blue against a dark rock; the boy's shirt as he perched high on the dangerous cliff.

'But he's dead,' Holly said. She heard the body smack against the water, she saw the blurred shape and the spread-eagled arms. 'No, forget I said it. It's impossible. How can there be a link between Daniel and the person in the cottage?'

Belinda and Tracy frowned. 'Yes, forget it. It's

74

just a coincidence,' Belinda agreed. They bent to pick up the the barrel.

'Too bad, I thought you were on to something there,' Tracy said. 'But you're right. Loads of people wear denim shirts. It doesn't mean a thing.'

Daniel was dead. The police had failed to find anything in the lake. The latest news was that they were appealing on the local radio for his relatives to come forward.

Holly nodded. On the whole, she was glad to push the memory of the fatal fall to the back of her mind once more. They had enough trouble to solve the new mystery of the cottage. 'Maybe we ought to write some of this down when we get back,' she suggested. 'In the Mystery Club notebook, so we don't overlook anything important.'

Belinda and Tracy nodded.

They trudged on through the rain, deep in thought.

7 Blue denim

Belinda, Tracy and Holly were so curious about the mystery surrounding Rover's Cottage that they rushed to carry, haul, slide and shove the hateful oil-drum round the lake. They arrived back at the Hall, arms and legs aching, loathing the very sight of the dented and bashed up object.

'Well done.' Jo Thomas raised the sash window in her office. She leaned out to congratulate them. 'You're back in record time. I'll have to tell Mike!'

Tracy grinned. 'Where is he?'

'Still down at the lake, I expect. Why?' Jo leaned on the windowsill, watching them store the barrel in its corner of the yard.

'We wanted to ask if we could go down into the village.' Tracy wiped her face with the front of her shirt.

Jo smiled. 'Well, in his absence, I think it's fair enough for me to give you permission.'

'Great!' Holly headed straight for the gate, followed by Belinda and Tracy.

'No, no!' Jo called them back. 'You need a shower and a change of clothes first. *Then* a trip to the village. OK?'

They turned in their tracks and trudged back into the Hall.

'Five minutes!' Belinda challenged, as they grabbed their towels and headed for the showers. 'Meet you back here in five minutes flat!'

'You're on!' They raced after her.

'Anyone would think the village was going to melt away like snow,' Jo observed. She raised her eyebrows as she bumped into them once more, showered and ready to go. 'But it'll still be there in half an hour's time!'

They laughed. The day was turning out the way they wanted it at last. It was late afternoon and they had a line of investigation to follow in the village shop. They set off, determined to find out who Mike had been searching for at the cottage, and, if possible, why. Even the clouds were lifting, and a watery sun was beginning to shine through.

They jogged down the road, across a field towards the river bank and followed the footpath into Butterpike village. It was a long, winding street of slate houses, standing grey-green in the

77

sunshine. They passed the whitewashed pub and an old church opposite. Then they headed towards a post-box at the roadside, the site of the village shop.

They stopped at last to read the sign over the window: 'Cordingley's General Stores'. The shelves inside were stacked with tins, packets, fresh fruit and vegetables and newspapers.

'Ready?' Belinda asked. She pressed her face against the door pane, looking for signs of life inside.

Holly looked up at the sign. 'It has to be worth a try!' she said eagerly.

A shop bell rang as Tracy pushed the door. A small, stout man in a fawn cardigan came out of the back room. 'Yes?' he asked suspiciously, as if customers were a rarity round these parts.

Belinda's eyes got used to the gloom of the tiny shop. She spotted the ice-cream fridge. 'Three vanilla tubs!' she said on the spur of the moment. 'Please!' She gave the shopkeeper a winning smile.

'Three, you say?' The old man put a hand up to his ear.

'Yes, please!' Belinda was still on her best behaviour. 'And three cans of Coke, please!'

Tracy and Holly stood at her shoulder and took their ice-cream tubs from old Mr Cordingley.

'Three?' he repeated. He picked up a pencil to jot down prices on a scrap of paper. 'Now, let's see, I'm getting low on Coke.' He shuffled along behind the counter, mumbling away.

'I suppose you sell a lot of it?' Belinda asked chattily. She pointed out the half-empty space on the shelf where the cans of Coke were stacked.

'Oh, yes. All the youngsters seem to like it.' He fumbled towards the back of the shelf.

Belinda went on chatting. 'And do you sell the six-packs as well?' she asked.

'What?' he said sharply, his hand to his ear. 'You say you want a six-pack now?'

'Yes, we might as well!' Holly nudged Belinda. 'We're extra thirsty, so we'll have six!'

'Well, you're out of luck!' the shopkeeper barked back. 'I don't stock 'em. Never have. No room for 'em!' He stood, arm poised by the shelf.

'Oh well, just three single cans, please.' Holly sighed. She felt the smile fall from her face as she dug into her pocket for some change.

Tracy took the cans. 'Have a nice day,' she said brightly to the old man as they made their exit, to the high ring of the shop bell.

'Hmm.' Belinda frowned as they stood outside. She ate her ice-cream. 'It seemed like a good idea at the time.'

'It was,' Holly commiserated. 'Only, it doesn't get us very far.' Cars whizzed up and down the narrow street. She noticed a red one speed by, then a blue one turning into the pub carpark.

'The Cross Keys.' Tracy could read its bright new sign from a distance of fifty metres. 'Hey, the Cross Keys!' Her face lit up again. 'Come on, what are we waiting for?'

Holly and Belinda followed her down the street.

'We'll try here!' Tracy was already through the door into the bar. 'You can buy Coke at a pub, can't you?'

She rushed in and caught the barmaid's attention, then came straight to the point. 'Hello, I wonder if you could help? We're looking for someone,' she explained. The middle-aged woman behind the bar was cheerful-looking. She was wiping glasses and putting them back on a shelf. 'Someone who might have come in here to buy a dozen cans of Coke, say yesterday or the day before.'

The barmaid put her tongue in her cheek and tilted her head backwards. 'Oh well, I'd remember that all right,' she said. 'A dozen sounds like a lot to me. But no, I can't recall . . .' She put her tea-towel down on the bar top and gave a little laugh. 'But then, I wouldn't, would I?'

'Why not?' Holly was puzzled.

'Because I've just had two days off!'

'Oh!' Holly's shoulders sagged. Another dead-end.

'But I take it it's important?' The woman eyed them carefully.

'It is.' Holly decided that honesty was the best policy. 'We're trying to find out who's been squatting in an old shepherd's cottage. We think he might be injured, and he might need help.' She decided to keep her explanation simple and not mention Mike Sandford's interrupted search.

'And it's someone with a thirst, you say?' Luckily, the barmaid seemed to be the sort who would soon tune in to a mystery like this. 'You don't mean Rover's Cottage, by any chance?' She leaned her head to one side. 'Only, I heard Colin say he thought there might be someone up there, living rough.'

'Who's Colin?' Tracy jumped in with a quick question.

'He's the landlord here. He was serving behind the bar during my days off. Just a second, I'll go and get him for you.' The woman disappeared from sight, leaving them standing impatiently in the cosy, red-carpeted room.

Holly looked excitedly at the other two. 'What's the betting we get a description now?'

But Colin wasn't the observant type, they soon discovered. He came into the bar in his off-duty slippers and an old grey sweater. He *ummed* and *aahed*. Yes, there had been someone who'd bought two six-packs of Coke. But no, he couldn't remember much about him. A youngish kid, scruffy-looking. That's what made him think he was probably living rough, and kids often chose Rover's Cottage to hole up in. He'd mentioned it to Lorna.

'Yes, they already know that,' the barmaid prompted. 'But these three want to know what he looked like.'

The landlord shrugged. 'Average. All kids look the same to me these days. Taller than me, skinnier than me, worse luck!' He patted his belly.

'Dark or fair?' Holly asked.

'Mousy. More dark than fair, I suppose.' Colin drummed his fingers on the copper bar top. 'Listen, Lorna, I forgot to mention; there's a group out in the garden who just ordered sandwiches for three. I've left them high and dry out there.'

Holly could see that they'd outstayed their welcome, but she persisted. 'You're sure you can't remember anything else about this particular kid? What he was wearing, for instance?'

Colin had already turned to go into the kitchen.

'The usual. Jeans. A scruffy denim shirt. I remember that much.' He shrugged, then disappeared.

'Denim!' Belinda breathed that word again.

Quickly Holly thanked Lorna. They backed out.

'I hope you manage to find him!' she called out cheerfully as they closed the door.

'So, he came here. He bought the Coke. He's darkish, tallish and scruffy. What else?' Tracy tried to map out what they'd learned.

'He's not known round here,' Holly pointed out. 'Or else even Colin would have recognised him!'

Belinda smiled. 'That's not bad for a start. Probably the next thing to do is to head back to the cottage, to see what else we can find.'

'What if he's still there?' Tracy asked. 'He'll probably just take off again, and we won't be any the wiser.'

They had rounded the corner of the pub into a trellis of rambling pink roses and a wooden archway that led into a quaint lawned back garden.

Suddenly Tracy stopped. She ducked down behind the rose hedge.

'What is it?' Holly had ducked too, pulling Belinda down with her.

'Not what; who!' Tracy whispered. 'Look at the far table, over in the corner. Do you see who I see?'

They peeped through a mass of green leaves, thorns and pink petals. Huddled at a round wrought-iron table, in close conversation, was Mike Sandford, with Tony Carter and Rob Slingsby, the two careworkers who had been in charge of Daniel.

'I didn't know they knew one another!' Holly gasped. 'Mike never mentioned it to the police or anyone!'

'Well, they do now,' Belinda said.

The men were so caught up in their conversation that the three girls were able to edge along the far side of the hedge, creeping closer, until the words came through loud and clear.

'Amsterdam,' Rob Slingsby said.

Tony Carter took up the explanation in a low, secretive voice. 'They know how to cut and polish in Amsterdam. That's why I took them there in the first place.'

Mike nodded. 'We'll soon see. But when exactly?'

'We're sailing back to Zeebrugge tonight. We make the same connection in Amsterdam, complete the deal, arrive back at midday tomorrow.' Rob Slingsby laid it out carefully, but the excitement in his voice was unmistakable. He took off his round glasses and polished them on a tissue.

Then he fixed them back on the bridge of his nose.

Tracy frowned. 'What on earth are they talking about?' she whispered.

Holly put a finger to her lips. 'I don't know,' she muttered. 'But it doesn't sound like they're planning a holiday!'

Belinda agreed. 'But they're not even supposed to know each other!' she said again.

Tony Carter stopped talking as Lorna came out with drinks and a plateful of sandwiches. He took a big bite, then spoke through the crumbs. 'From now on, we have to keep Martin well out of this!' he warned. 'We don't want any more trouble from that direction!'

'Don't worry, I'll fix it.' Mike looked up uneasily. Holly, Tracy and Belinda ducked down low. 'Martin is history, OK? Or will be, as soon as I get my hands on the little swine!'

'When will that be?' Rob inspected his sandwich as the girls risked another look through the hedge. He took a small, precise bite.

'Tonight.'

Rob and Tony Carter nodded. 'You'll sort it out for good this time?' Carter insisted. 'Remember, he's like a cat. He's got more than one life!'

They laughed at the in-joke.

'No problem,' Mike said. 'Tonight's the night!'

Rob Slingsby finished his sandwich, downed his beer, then wiped his mouth. 'Well, that's down to you,' he said. 'We'll be elsewhere. Now all we need to do is fix a time and place for our next meeting.'

'As long as you're sure about Martin?' Carter seemed less cool about things than Slingsby. He loosened his collar and tie as he spoke.

'Look, just forget him, will you!' Mike turned on him. 'We've stitched him up good and proper already, so he can't go squealing to the police or anyone. Now all I have to do is finish the job.'

'OK, OK, you two!' Slingsby broke the row that was brewing by standing up and pushing his chair back from the table. 'A time and place?' He pressed for the information from Mike.

'Not here,' came the reply. 'It's a small world, everyone knows everyone else. No, let's make it Windermere, twelve o'clock Friday morning. Meet me at the Coffee Pot. It's a cafe on the waterfront, facing the jetty where they moor the steamboats. You can't miss it.' Mike stood up, as tall as Slingsby and broader across the shoulders. The girls noticed a wide strapping of sticking plaster across the cut on Slingby's arm as the two men shook hands.

'You'll bring the items with you, of course?' Mike reminded him.

Slingsby nodded. 'Naturally.'

Through the rose bush, Holly, Tracy and Belinda saw them head towards the garden gate, out on to the main street. Holly tugged at Tracy's sleeve, warning her to edge still further out of sight. But Tracy stumbled and overbalanced into the hedge. Its branches shook. Pink petals cascaded all around. Mike Sandford stopped in his tracks.

'What was that?' he snapped. He strode across the lawn towards them.

'Oh, no!' Holly gasped. They froze like startled rabbits.

'Pretend we're just casually passing!' Belinda hissed. She hauled Tracy out of the rose hedge.

Holly coughed and brushed petals from Tracy's hair. Mike had turned and spotted them.

'Not you three again!' he exclaimed.

Slingsby and Carter ran through the gate to cut off the girls' retreat.

'We – we've just been to the shop,' Belinda stammered. She tried to lighten things up. 'Fancy meeting you here!'

This time Mike didn't even bother to hide his annoyance. 'Look, I won't have people spying on me,' he said. 'Is that clear?'

87

They nodded, heads down, preparing to take what they knew must come next.

'Get yourselves back to the Hall and wait there for me,' he instructed. 'And don't expect to get away with this,' he warned. 'Because this time you've just gone too far!'

8   Set-up

Holly, Tracy and Belinda jogged back to Butterpike Hall, dreading the trouble they'd have to face for spying on Mike.

'They are *not* supposed to know one another!' Holly repeated. It was surprise at seeing Mike, Carter and Slingsby sitting together over a drink that had made them careless.

'But they sure do,' Tracy said. 'Maybe it really is time we wrote this all down in the notebook?' she suggested.

'OK,' Holly agreed. 'I'll go straight up and get it from my locker when we get back.'

They ran on for a while, along the footpath, through the wood to the Hall. 'Look, can't we slow down just a teeny bit?' Belinda gasped. Jogging, like climbing, was something she didn't enjoy.

'No, let's get a move on,' Tracy insisted. 'Holly can grab the notebook and we can start work before Mike gets back.'

They hurried on, anxious to begin.

But when Mike arrived, he cornered them in the games room. He caught them off guard, and Holly had to snatch the Mystery Club's red notebook from Belinda to stuff it into her shirt pocket. Mike glanced suspiciously at her, leaned on the snooker table and fixed them with a cool stare. 'OK, you admit you were spying on me?' he asked.

'Not spying exactly.' Holly tried to stand up to him. 'It was more of an accident really. We weren't expecting to see you.' *Especially not with those other two*, she thought of adding.

'So it's normal behaviour to hide behind rose bushes, is it?' He raised both eyebrows, took up a snooker cue and examined the metal tip. Then he leaned forward and took a shot. A red ball cannoned into a pocket across the green baize.

Holly frowned and glanced at Tracy and Belinda. They stood uneasily by the window, awaiting the full force of Mike's anger, puzzled by his cool manner. After all, he'd warned them that they weren't going to get away with things this time.

But he went on expertly potting balls as he talked. 'I'm not really so frightening, am I?' He grinned. 'People don't usually take it into their heads to hide at the sight of me!'

'Tactical error!' Belinda admitted to Tracy out of the corner of her mouth. 'Why couldn't we look more casual?'

'Difficult when you've just fallen into a rose bush,' Tracy whispered back.

Holly stood wondering what Mike was up to now.

Mike moved round the table, lining up the black ball. He aimed. The cue cracked against the white ball, firing the black straight into a side pocket. He stood up, smiling. 'Listen,' he said in an ultra-reasonable tone. 'I know you three are always rooting around for some kind of mystery to solve. I expect you can't help it.'

The three girls braced themselves to meet his sarcastic stare. Why wasn't he yelling and shouting at them?

Mike leaned his cue against the table. 'But don't you think enough is enough?' He folded his arms. 'I mean, can't I even go for a quiet drink at the Cross Keys without being spied on?'

Holly cleared her throat and held her hands clasped behind her back. 'We were just surprised, that's all.'

'What by? That I meet some friends occasionally?'

'No. But we didn't realise you knew Mr Slingsby

91

and Mr Carter.' She steeled herself for his reaction.

Up went the eyebrows. A faint smile crept into his face. 'And that's a crime in your book, is it?'

'No, but . . .'

'Look, it's since the accident, that's all. We got together for a drink. All three of us felt pretty bad about the boy falling like that. We partly blamed ourselves.' Mike's expression was serious now, his voice quiet. 'We decided to keep in touch, see if the police come up with anything, and so on.'

Holly nodded. *It's possible*, she told herself. *But it doesn't really fit with the conversation we overheard.*

'Anyway,' Mike went on, 'it's given me the chance to clear the air with you. And I propose we forget what's just happened. Let's start afresh one more time, shall we?'

'OK,' Holly nodded. His mood swing still surprised her. She glanced again at the other two. 'Thanks,' she added.

He laughed. 'Not at all. When I came in it looked as if you were expecting the full works. You'd all gone pale! What did you expect; that I'd have you thrown off the course or something?' He headed for the door, still laughing.

'Oh, no!' Tracy shook her head. But she thought

she saw a veiled threat under the light-hearted remark.

'Well, I won't. Not this time!' he joked. He nodded back at them, then sauntered off. They heard him whistle as he went.

Belinda took a deep breath. 'What *is* going on?'

Tracy flicked the white ball thoughtfully across the green table. It ricochetted from a side cushion and rolled to a halt. 'Maybe he's an all-round nice guy, after all?'

'Maybe.' Belinda still felt relieved that he hadn't stormed on at them. She hated it when people shouted.

'Maybe not.' Holly unbuttoned her shirt pocket. She pulled out the Mystery Club's red notebook. 'How far did we get?' she asked, looking round.

'I'll just check it's all quiet out there.' Belinda went to the door. It was nearly time for the evening meal, so the corridor was almost deserted. 'OK!' She joined the others in a huddle, leaning forward against the table, heads down.

'Do we believe Mike Sandford?' Holly asked. She'd written the words earlier in capital letters, then divided her page in two. Now she wrote 'YES' at the head of the left-hand column, 'NO' on the right.

Tracy pointed to the left side. 'Yes, because it's

true. They _would_ all be upset about the boy's fall. Mike might want to keep in touch with the two careworkers.' Holly wrote this down. 'Yes, because he seems to be good at his job. Jo Thomas obviously likes having him as part of her team.' After this, Tracy was stuck.

'How about the 'NO' column?' Belinda asked. Then she launched into the new list. 'No, we don't believe him because those three seemed pretty pleased with themselves down at the pub. They didn't look like they were grief-stricken about the boy or anything.'

Holly nodded and continued to write. 'Yes, and they weren't slow to strike up that business deal since they first met on Monday,' she reminded them. 'All that stuff about Amsterdam!'

'Write it down!' Tracy began to sound excited. 'And was that deal as shady as it sounded?'

Holly glanced up. She bit at the end of the pen, frown lines knitting her brow. 'Amsterdam,' she said slowly. 'Cutting and polishing . . . Diamonds!'

'How come?' Belinda didn't see the connection.

'But that's it!' Holly exclaimed. 'I once saw a programme on TV. Amsterdam is famous for its diamond-cutting workshops. They import diamonds from Africa to cut and polish them into gems. Maybe that's what they were on about!'

'Africa?' Tracy took off on a new tack. 'Hey, isn't that where Mike went on safari? Maybe he's buying and selling diamonds now!'

They looked at one another, eyes glittering. Suddenly, the urgent conversation at the pub made sense.

'But there's no law against it, is there?' Tracy considered this new possibility. 'I mean, people can buy and sell diamonds, can't they?'

'If they can afford it,' Holly put in. 'But why would Mike still be working in an outdoor pursuits centre if he could make a living buying and selling diamonds instead?'

'Maybe he only just hit lucky?' Tracy suggested. She studied the two columns in their red notebook. They were pretty evenly balanced. For a few seconds, the girls fell silent.

'Let's go back and think about the cottage,' Holly suggested. 'Let's try a fresh angle.'

'OK, firstly, Mike broke down the door,' Belinda said. 'Next, he was looking for someone; not us. Third, he was angry. That's three more things for your "NO" column.'

'That "someone" was injured,' Tracy reminded them. 'And Mike had come to get him, for sure. You remember what he said?'

Holly recalled it word for word. 'He said, "I

know you're up there, you little swine!"' She heard the phrase echo inside her head. She'd heard it more recently. When? Where? 'Little swine,' she repeated.

'Martin!' It clicked in Tracy's mind. 'That's what Mike called the mysterious Martin when he was talking to Slingsby and Carter. "Little swine", he said. "Martin is history, OK? Or will be, as soon as I get my hands on the little swine!"'

'Hey, a breakthrough!' Belinda jabbed her finger at the 'NO' column. 'Write it down, Holly! Mike's after someone called Martin who was hiding up at Rover's Cottage! My getting lost and going there first must have scared this Martin off. That's why Mike's been so mad at us ever since!'

Holly scribbed it all down. 'So, who *is* Martin?' she asked. Tracy was still rolling the white ball round the table as she concentrated on the problem. Belinda had gone to the window to stare out across the lawn to the oak trees and the fellside beyond. 'We know from the landlord at the Cross Keys that he's a kid, he's skinny, he's darkish. He's injured in some way, but probably not badly.'

'He's scared,' Tracy added.

'And Mike has "stitched him up" already.' Belinda brought this phrase back to mind.

'Injured. Dark. Tall. And skinny.' Holly repeated

the landlord's vague description. It too jogged at her memory. 'You know, that just about fits the description of the boy who fell. Daniel was tall and dark, wasn't he?' She tailed off, unsure how to go on. It didn't add up. Daniel was dead.

'No, hold on!' Belinda jumped down from the windowsill. She went to grab the notebook from Holly. 'What if Daniel didn't really die in the lake? What if he fought himself free behind those rocks?'

Tracy nodded. 'Could be. We heard lots of shouting and stuff.'

'And Rob Slingsby came back with that cut on his arm,' Holly remembered. 'Even Tony Carter looked as if he'd been roughed up a bit. He'd lost his jacket. His shirt was pulled out all over the place!'

Belinda took up the theory. 'So Daniel fought the three of them off. He made his getaway, up the fell to the cottage.' She paused again. 'Where does that leave us?'

'It leaves us with a body still falling into the lake. A body they never found,' Tracy said. She whisked the ball across the table, watching it shoot off the far cushion. It rolled to a slow stop, teetered on the edge of a corner pocket, then dropped in.

'What if it was a set-up?' Holly cried. 'What if

Daniel didn't fall after all? Maybe they made the whole thing up! I know, it sounds crazy, and I don't know *how* they did it, not yet! But maybe that's what Mike meant about "stitching him up"!'

'But he was talking about Martin, not Daniel!' Belinda pointed out.

The two names jostled and jumbled in Holly's mind. *Martin, Daniel. Daniel, Martin.* 'Daniel Martyn!' she cried. 'Daniel *is* Martin! They're the same person after all!'

It was like fog lifting from the mountains. It was like being able to see clearly into the far distance. Belinda and Tracy congratulated Holly. The clues made sense at last.

'But why?' Belinda asked. They were getting changed in the dorm after a hurried supper in the cafeteria. Everyone had gone off their separate ways after Jo had announced a free evening. 'Why would Mike Sandford need to pretend that Daniel Martyn had died in the fall?' She slipped her green sweat-shirt over her head. It would be cool high up on the fell at this time in the evening.

'That's what we need to find out!' Tracy said. She stood ready and waiting by the door. 'Someone bring a torch, OK?'

Holly grabbed one from her bedside table. 'We

might not need it, but it's better to be sure. Ready!'

'Do we plan to storm up there without trying to hide where we're going?' Belinda asked.

'No point creeping about,' Holly said. Her nerves were taut and strained. Mike Sandford's phrase came back to spook her. 'Tonight's the night!' he'd promised his business partners. 'The main thing is to get up to Rover's Cottage before Mike does. Anyway, what could he do to Daniel in front of three witnesses?'

Belinda struggled to find the breath to speak as they ran uphill. 'He could order us back to the Hall again for a start.'

'It's our night off,' Tracy said. 'We can go where we like. Holly's right; we just need to be there, even if it scares Daniel off again. At least Mike won't be able to get his hands on him.'

'Does he know Mike's still after him, I wonder?' Holly asked. So far, the boy had seemed good at making his quick getaways. 'I only hope he's keeping a good lookout. Maybe if we can get to talk to him, we can warn him about what's going on. He might not even know that he's supposed to be dead!'

Soon the sign for Rover's Cottage came into view, nestled deep in the heather and fern of the hillside. Then they spotted the ramshackle house, overgrown and looking as deserted as ever. They ran down the path into the hollow, on the lookout for signs of life.

'Hello?' Holly put her knuckles to the broken door and knocked quietly. 'Hello, Daniel?' They'd been quick to get up here but had they been quick enough?

There was no reply. The door creaked on its remaining hinge and swung open. They ventured inside 'Hello?' Holly said again. Something clattered in the sitting-room. Something blundered at the door.

Tracy sprang forward and pressed herself to the wall, hidden from the view of whoever was in there. She gestured at Holly and Belinda to keep out of the way. Slowly, she eased her head round the doorway.

'Be careful!' Belinda warned from behind, ready to pull Tracy back out of danger.

Holly tensed up, alert to the smallest sound. With a bit of luck, it would be three against one. They crouched, ready and waiting.

There was a face with wild yellow eyes. A black, bony face with horns.

The sheep charged again at the doorway, its hooves clattering. It dashed into the hall and barged at Belinda, knocking her sideways. Then it made for the square of daylight and out into the fresh air.

'A sheep!' Holly grinned with relief. 'Looks like no one else is around! Come on!'

She led the way into the kitchen. 'Is anyone here?' she called. Ashes from the fire lay dead in the grate. The room was deserted.

Belinda drew breath. 'All neat and tidy.' She noticed that the cans and biscuits had been cleared away. The white bowl stood empty in the sink.

'Yep, looks like he's gone all right.' Tracy tried the window. It was locked from the inside. A green bottle covered in candlewax stood neatly on the windowsill.

'At least he didn't have to leave in a hurry,' Holly said. 'That's a good sign. It looks like he packed up and left before Mike caught up with him. We hope!' She went out and climbed the dusty stairway, to explore the upstairs rooms.

Belinda stayed at the bottom, peering round, almost expecting to see Mike's face in a window, or staring down at them from the top of the stairs. Dusk was drawing in. She was glad they'd brought the torch.

Holly's footsteps echoed across the bedroom floor. She came and looked over the banister. 'No sign of anything up here,' she reported.

101

Tracy nodded. 'I wonder where he went.' She sighed. 'It means we'll have to try and pick up the trail again, I suppose.'

'So we can warn him and tell him we're on his side,' Belinda agreed.

'*Are* we on his side?' Holly came slowly downstairs. 'Are we on the side of a thief? They were taking him to a detention centre, remember?'

They walked together down the hallway. Tracy closed the broken door behind them.

'Hmm.' Belinda took off her glasses. Their investigation had come a long way in a short time, but there was the boy himself to consider. She swung her glasses to and fro. 'He didn't *look* like a thief,' she reminded them.

'And he hadn't been tried and found guilty, had he?' Tracy pointed out. 'Isn't he innocent until proven guilty?'

'*And*,' Belinda said with added energy, 'remember how mad Mike was with Daniel when he broke into the cottage? What was behind all that, if he'd never set eyes on him before the accident? No, Mike's got something against Daniel that we don't know about.'

'Not yet,' Holly agreed. She marched ahead, out on to the open hillside. Below them, the lake looked silver-grey in the evening light. 'Right. We're on

Daniel's side! Even though there are still things about this whole set-up that don't make sense!'

They walked down the fell, back to the Hall, all the while keeping a look out for Mike Sandford and the mysterious, disappearing Daniel Martyn.

9 White water

Mike Sandford gave nothing away at breakfast the next morning. Holly studied his tanned face as he gave out instructions for the day.

'He looks OK to me!' Tracy whispered. 'Maybe we've been jumping the gun about all this,' She was reluctant to believe that Mike was mixed up in a shady deal involving diamonds. This morning, she was willing to think that he was the straightforward outdoors activity leader that everyone else assumed him to be.

'Uh-oh, Tracy's changing her mind,' Belinda warned. She stood in a group with Tracy, Holly, Steffie, Ollie and Mark, all eager to find out their day's activities. The others were having fun at Butterpike Hall; all except her. 'I'm telling you now,' she whispered, 'this is the last time you get me into a pair of walking boots in my life!' She groaned as she felt the tender spots on her heels and toes.

Holly grinned. But she was too busy studying Mike's face to pay much attention. *Maybe he does look a bit strained,* she thought. A small nerve flickered above his left eye, making his lid jump and twitch. But he seemed calm as he went about doing his job.

'Now,' he said, turning to the Mystery Club after dealing with Steffie and the two boys, 'I suppose you three have had enough fell-climbing and barrel-rolling for the time being?'

Before Holly had time to look for a hidden meaning, he went on smoothly.

'So today you can go white-water rafting with the others instead!'

In spite of their suspicions about Mike, Tracy jumped to her feet. 'Great!' She loved the idea of going out on to the fast-flowing river that fed the lake. She pictured having to steer a course between jagged rocks and struggling to stay upright in the water.

'He just wants to keep us away from the cottage from now on!' Belinda muttered to Holly. But they followed Mike down to a boatshed in the grounds, and listened carefully as he decribed how to manoeuvre the inflatable rafts out of the shed on to a trailer in the yard.

Soon, their own group, plus a second one

made up of Steffie, Ollie and Mark, piled into the Land-rover and set off across country to High Force, the place they'd seen on the map during their orienteering trek.

'Remember, keep these life-jackets on at all times,' Mike told them. They struggled into the orange plastic waistcoats as he handed them out to each person. They'd pulled up in a small carpark by the steep waterfall. 'You set off from here. You travel two kilometres downstream, and come ashore in the shallows at the edge of the lake.' He looked round. 'Now, this is a tough activity, and the timing is important. If you don't reach the lake exactly on time, we alert the rescue team from the Hall, in case there's been an accident.' He paused again. 'Anyone feel like backing out at this point?'

They all shook their heads. They stood under tall trees that clung to the river-bank, hearing the water roar and gush into a pool at the base of the fall. They felt the thrill of danger, the challenge of the unknown.

'It's very important to follow instructions!' Mike warned them. 'Stick together, three to each raft. If you come off, go with the current, don't fight it. The whole route should take about ten minutes. Then we pick up the rafts on the trailer, tow them back up, and start all over again!'

Holly's group watched as Ollie, Mark and Steffie took to the water first. Spray freshened their faces, sunlight dappled the trees. 'This will be fantastic!' Tracy said, all other thoughts put to one side. 'This is what we came here for!'

'Right!' Belinda raised her eyebrows and laughed. 'We came here to get soaking wet and risk life and limb. And they call it fun!'

'Softie!' Holly gave a gentle push.

'I know, I admit it,' Belinda mumbled. She sighed at the task ahead of them.

But soon even Belinda rose to the challenge and began to help Tracy and Holly to haul their raft down to the water's edge. The current had taken swift hold of Steffie's raft as Mike stood on the bank and let them go. They swirled into the white water at the centre of the stream, and, kneeling in the middle, they began to paddle furiously. Soon, they rounded the bend, out of sight.

Mike timed things precisely on his watch, noting when Steffie's group should arrive at the lake. Then he turned to Holly's group. 'Ready? Remember, I'll be waiting down there to pick you up!'

They nodded and stepped with trembling legs on to the raft. They knelt quickly, paddles at the ready. Mike released them. They were off. Cold water foamed all round, the raft tipped, they steadied it with the oars. Steering between two huge boulders, they let the current take them.

Between steep white cliffs, down narrow, racing channels, they swerved and balanced. The water roared. It slid like a dark, glinting snake, many metres deep. It gushed between sharp rocks. 'Watch out!' Holly yelled. They ducked beneath an overhanging branch. Then they battled to stay clear of the bank.

'Isn't this great?' Tracy grinned in the face of the ice-cold spray and roaring current.

'Tracy, lean to the right!' Belinda yelled. The raft swept towards a huge boulder, smooth as a whale's back. Belinda felt her stomach lurch as they plunged wide of the rock.

'That was close!' Holly admitted. Her knuckles were white with clinging to the hand-holds; her whole body ached from the battle to stay upright.

At last, tired and triumphant, they came clear of the rapids and drifted into the still, clear water of the lake.

'We did it!' Belinda leapt off the raft. 'We did it! That was absolutely brilliant!'

Steffie laughed as she ran towards them. 'Wasn't that just the *best* experience?'

Holly and Tracy followed Belinda on to the shore,

dragging their raft. 'No, the best bit is we get to do it again!' Tracy grinned. Mike's Land-rover was parked by the lakeside, with him sitting inside nodding his approval.

They loaded the trailer and rode back up to High Force. Then they worked together to unhook the rafts under Mike's expert eye.

'This should keep you out of mischief,' he said to Holly with a smile as they stood and watched Steffie's group set off once more. He had one foot on the side runner of the Land-rover, getting ready to drive down to the lake again. 'Remember, timing is important. If you're late, we'll assume the worst. Give the others exactly five minutes start, then follow straight on.' He started up the engine and roared off down the track.

A minute went by, with nothing but the rush and gurgle of the water to disturb the silence. Belinda kept an impatient check on her watch. Holly glanced up the waterfall at the mass of water tumbling down. She looked a second time. Had she spotted a blurred shape, a movement in the green leaves of the overhanging branches? She couldn't be sure. 'What was that?' She pointed quickly up the side of the waterfall.

Belinda glanced up. 'What? I can't see anything.'

Holly scrambled on to a rock to see if she could catch a second glimpse of the mysterious figure.

'Hey!' Tracy called from the water's edge. 'Where are you off to?' She held tight to the raft, still eager to get under way.

'I'm sure I saw someone!' Holly was convinced that the figure was human; that it had spotted them down below and darted under cover. 'Someone in blue!' she told them.

Belinda shot her a look. 'Where?'

'Up there! He's gone now!'

'No, there he is!' Belinda pointed along a ridge at one side of the waterfall. 'I saw him too! Now he's gone again!'

'Hey, you two!' Tracy struggled on by herself. The raft had drifted wide of the bank and was caught in the current. She'd been tugged two or three steps into the stream. Now she clung on, leaning backwards, shouting for help.

Holly and Belinda ran to lend a hand. 'Let's pull it ashore for a second!' Holly yelled above the roar of the water. She and Belinda succeeded in dragging the raft clear. 'I want to go and take a look!'

'We don't have time!' Tracy protested. 'Remember, Mike wants us to arrive on time.'

'Yes we do! It won't take long. Come on!' Holly

let go of the beached raft and pleaded with Tracy to follow her hunch.

'OK!' Tracy agreed. 'But we'd better be quick.'

Then all three ran to the waterfall. They began to haul themselves up the rocks, covering a distance of about twenty metres in the space of one minute. Drenched with spray, breathing hard, they took a breather on a narrow ledge.

'What was it?' Tracy gasped. 'What did you two spot up here?' She eased the straps of her life-jacket and crouched back against the rock face.

'I don't know for sure. All I know is, I saw something blue!' Holly told her.

'Me too!' Belinda nodded hard. She glanced down at the dizzy drop. Water cascaded into the deep pool. 'You don't think it could be Daniel?'

'If it was, it was the most alive looking corpse I've ever seen!' Holly muttered. She peered up through the wet green leaves. But there was no sign of movement up there now.

'Hey, look in here!' Tracy took hold of Belinda's arm. She made her peer into the dark space at the back of the waterfall. 'There's a kind of cave. Look!'

Holly too crept forward to investigate. They all stared along the ledge. Behind the curtain of rushing water, they could make out that the ledge widened out into a natural cave, cut deep into the rock. Tracy went down on all fours. 'I'm going to take a look,' she whispered. 'It's just a hunch, but . . .'

She crawled forwards, hidden by the fall, careful not to slip on the mossy green surface. When she could turn sideways and crawl into the cave, she found it was dry and clean. 'Someone could live in here!' she called out. 'Come and look!'

Cautiously, Belinda and Holly followed her. Soon they were all squatting safely under the domed roof.

'Good, isn't it?' Tracy looked all round.

Holly agreed. 'This would be a great place for someone to hide!' Her eyes sparkled in the gloom as she searched for any sign of life.

'The sand on the floor's nice and dry.' Belinda ran her fingers along the soft surface. 'Hey, and look; there's a ledge back here for storing things!' She fumbled until her hand made contact with a smooth, cylindrical shape. She rolled it off the ledge.

They stared at the object in the palm of her hand. 'A can of Coke!' Tracy breathed.

Belinda went on searching the ledge. She felt further back. 'I can feel two more here, and some other stuff as well!' There were soft, flat packets,

112

and a heavy, long shape; maybe a scouting knife with its blade firmly closed. She turned to face Tracy and Holly.

'It's Daniel's new hiding-place!' Holly said.

'Phew! Pretty good!' Tracy looked out at the impenetrable curtain of water that covered the entrance to the cave. 'No one would guess he was here!'

'Except us,' Belinda said. 'Did he see us crawl in here?'

'Who knows?' Holly shrugged. 'It might scare him off again if he did.' She knew Daniel wouldn't stay in a place once he'd been disturbed. 'What should we do?' Time was running out; Mike would expect them to be shooting the rapids at this very minute.

'We're not helping him much, are we?' Belinda said her face serious. 'He must feel as if we're hounding him!'

'Yes, so this time we've got to show him we want to help,' Tracy agreed. This was too good a chance to miss.

'How?' Belinda looked round the rough walls of the cave for inspiration. Seconds ticked on. They'd soon be in bad trouble, if they didn't set off on their raft.

It came to Holly in a flash. 'Got it!' She moved

Tracy and Belinda to one side and grabbed a piece of brushwood lying by the cave entrance. Swiftly she swept the sandy floor clear of their footprints. Then she picked up a small, sharp stick. She leaned over the sand and began to write.

The message was bold and clear in the sand: 'WE WANT TO HELP – MEET US HERE!'

Holly leaned back. 'Will he be able to read it?' she asked.

'Sure.' Tracy nodded. 'Now let's go, or else Mike will be sending out the rescue team! We're really late!'

She led the way along the ledge, back into broad daylight. Then they scrambled and slid back down the rock, jumped on to the pebbles and ran for the raft. They leapt on to it, sending it rocking crazily away from the bank. The fast current caught them. They were off, leaving behind their message to Daniel. The sound of the water filled their ears, as they rushed downstream once more.

10 Waiting game

'What kept you three?' Mike Sandford asked. He shot a suspicious glance at Holly, Tracy and Belinda as they clambered off the raft into the shallow water at the edge of the lake. A breeze blew through his dark-blue waterproof jacket. He stood, feet firmly planted on the pebbly shore, frowning at them.

'Nothing!' Holly felt her answer come a fraction of a second too quickly and she blushed. 'We just didn't time it well, that's all.'

'You had us worried,' he said. 'What happened? Can't any of you tell the time?' He strode towards them, past Steffie, Ollie and Mark.

'Well, they're here now, and they're safe,' Steffie pointed out.

Tracy nodded. 'That's right.'

But Mike ignored everyone. 'What held you up this time?' he insisted. He stared at Belinda. 'You didn't get lost again, did you?'

Belinda couldn't tell whether or not he was joking. She blushed. 'I do have a terrible sense of direction,' she agreed, ready to accept the blame.

Holly gave her a secret grin.

But Mike had already switched his attention to Tracy's life-jacket. 'Didn't I tell you to keep that thing properly fastened at all times?'

Tracy remembered loosening it during the climb up to Daniel's cave. She hadn't had time to tighten it again. 'Sorry,' she mumbled.

'Sorry's not enough if you're swept away by the current and your life-jacket's not secure.' He studied each of their faces. 'So what did keep you?' It was clear from his expression that he wasn't going to accept vague excuses.

'It was my fault,' Holly said. 'I wasn't ready to set off.'

'You don't say!' Mike fixed his gaze on her.

'I wandered off for a few minutes, that's all.'

'I thought you knew always to stick together?'

'We did,' Holly nodded. She could feel Ollie and Mark staring at her without much sympathy. She knew she was ruining their day. Only Steffie looked sorry that Holly was in trouble.

Mike sighed. 'Look, this isn't a funfair, you know. These activities must go exactly to plan, otherwise they're dangerous.' He held up both hands to stem protests. 'They're only safe if you follow instructions; if you stick to what you've been told. Like, wear your life-jackets at all times, keep to time and stay together! Then there's no problem. But if you do what you three have just done, it messes things up completely. I was on the point of calling out a rescue team from the centre!'

'We're sorry. We truly are.' Holly knew she was to blame. But following Daniel's trail had been vital.

Mike turned away. 'Get in the car!' he ordered. 'All of you. We'll go straight back and let Jo sort this out. I can't risk another run down the river.'

'But you said we could go again!' Mark cut in.

Mike strode to the Land-rover. 'Yes, but that was before these three messed up again. Blame them.' He jumped in and started the engine.

Mark and Ollie shot dark glances at the girls. 'Typical!' Ollie grumbled, as he hauled a raft on to the trailer. 'Now you have to start ruining things for other people!'

They climbed into the back of the car, stony-faced.

'Lay off, Ollie!' Steffie warned. 'Can't you see it's bad enough?'

Holly, Belinda and Tracy sat silently in the back,

guilty and troubled, as the Land-rover lurched up the rocky track.

Back at Butterpike Hall, the three girls unloaded the rafts, while Steffie, Ollie and Mark got the afternoon off to go swimming in the lake. 'You three, stay here,' Mike told them sternly. 'Wait until I've seen Jo and we've decided what to do with you, OK!' Then he strode out of the yard.

Belinda felt her heart sink. 'Do you think he knows something?' she whispered. The empty, leaded windows of the Hall glinted in the afternoon sun, but the girls stood in shadow, chilled and nervous.

Holly shook her head. 'He may *suspect* something, but he can't *know* that we found the cave and left Daniel a message!' she said. 'I don't suppose he even knows about the cave.'

'So what do we do now?' Tracy asked.

'Wait,' Holly told her. 'It's all we can do!' Wait to see what Daniel did when he found their message traced in sand. Wait to see what action Mike Sandford would take against them now.

They idled away the afternoon in the games room. Belinda had a half-hearted game of table-tennis with Holly. Tracy practised at the snooker table. The time crawled by.

'I wonder where he is now?' Belinda sighed. She stood holding her tennis bat, but her face was glued to the window pane.

'Who? Daniel?' Holly was trying to think ahead. How could they arrange to go out and meet him as promised, now that they were confined to the grounds?

'No, Mike.' Belinda said. 'I wonder if he's spoken to Jo about us yet. What do you suppose she'll say?'

Tracy shrugged. 'Who knows? He's bound to make everything sound real bad!' She imitated Mike's deep voice. '"They disobeyed orders again! They're a disaster! And bad for the morale of the other kids! They'll have to go!"'

Holly smiled. 'Don't exaggerate.'

'"Rank disobedience! I won't have it!"' Tracy mimicked. 'Can't you just imagine it?'

'Don't!' Holly groaned.

'Anyone would think this was the army!' Belinda grumbled.

'You love it really,' Holly teased. 'Just think how good all this fresh air and exercise is for you!'

'Who are you kidding? I'm missing all the best TV programmes while I'm out in that horrible fresh air,' Belinda groaned. 'I had to get my dad to promise to tape them!'

'Shh!' Tracy warned. 'Here comes someone

119

now!' She shot back to the table-tennis table, as if she'd never left it. 'Play!' she told Holly. 'Look innocent!'

Jo poked her auburn head through the doorway. 'Hello, you three! You're back early!' She glanced at her watch. 'Have any of you seen Mike?'

Holly breathed a sigh of relief, though she knew the reprieve was only going to be short-lived. At least Jo still looked on them with friendly eyes. 'Not for a while,' she replied. For a moment, she was tempted to spill everything out to Jo before Mike could give his version of events. But she hesitated too long and missed her chance.

'I just wanted to have a word with him about something,' Jo said. 'I'm in a bit of a rush right now, but would you tell him if you see him, please?' She smiled pleasantly then dashed out again.

Tracy swallowed hard. 'I can't bear this!' she moaned. 'This waiting just kills me!'

Holly and Belinda nodded. 'If only we could *do* something,' Belinda agreed.

'There's one thing we could do,' Holly suggested. 'I could go and fetch our notebook. We can add the things we've seen today. Daniel's cave, and so on.'

Tracy nodded. 'Good idea.'

So Holly dashed up the old carved staircase, along the wide gallery to the girls' dormitory. The Hall was deserted; all the other groups on the course were still out abseiling, climbing and mountain biking. Quickly Holly passed the empty shower-room and the linen store, until she came to the dormitory. Then she stopped dead in her tracks.

Something was different. She looked all round, an uneasy feeling growing inside her. A book she'd left lying open on the pillow was closed, and she was certain that Tracy hadn't left her locker door open as it was now. The white curtains billowed at the open windows, shoes lay kicked off under beds. Perhaps she was imagining things; this was the normal chaos of the girls' dormitory.

But as Holly went to collect the Mystery Club's notebook from her own bedside locker, she grew more certain that some things had been deliberately disturbed. Her hairbrush was knocked on to the floor, a box of tissues was turned upside down. Who had been here? What were they looking for?

Nervously she opened the shallow drawer of her locker. She felt inside and put her hand on the flat, square shape of the vital notebook. She pulled it out. It fell open at the page which read 'Do we believe Mike Sandford?', more easily than it had done before. It seemed as if someone had forced the spine back at this particular page.

For a moment, Holly checked her suspicions. Surely not. Surely no one would risk sneaking a look in her own private drawer. But Mike had spotted the notebook when he came into the games room. Had he seen her shove it quickly into her pocket? What if he had crept in here and found the evidence that they were on to him right before his eyes?

Holly gasped and leaned her head back against the wall. Then she closed the book and set off with it across the dormitory, out into the corridor, past the linen store. If it was true, then Mike must know how dangerous they were to him now, and he also knew they still hadn't cracked the full case. Before they did, she realised he would do everything he could to get rid of them. Swiftly she ran downstairs.

'Where were you?' Tracy jumped down from the windowsill in the games room as Holly rushed in. 'What kept you? We've been waiting ages!'

'And we just saw Mike!' Belinda reported. 'On his way down the corridor to Jo's room. He looked terrible. You can hear raised voices in there now!'

Holly groaned. 'I think I know why!' She held up the notebook. 'I've no proof, but I think he sneaked into our empty dorm and found this!'

Belinda and Tracy stared, taken aback by the latest development.

'He's in Jo's office right now, telling her how useless we are, trying his best to get rid of us!' Holly pictured the scene.

'And all we can do is hang around waiting for it to happen!' Tracy wailed.

At last they heard a door open and close.

'That's Mike leaving Jo's office!' Belinda guessed.

'What now?' Tracy stood frozen to the spot.

'Just wait!' Holly insisted again.

The office door opened.

'That's Jo now!' Belinda predicted. 'What are we going to tell her?'

Holly thought fast. 'Nothing,' she said.

'What? You mean, we're just going to let them throw us off the course? Can't we tell her what we suspect about Daniel and Mike?'

Holly shook her head. 'Where's our evidence? Where's the motive? Who would believe us?'

So they stood in silent dread. Jo appeared in the doorway dressed in a black track suit. She looked grave as she approached.

'*Now* I understand why you were back early,'

she began. She paced around the snooker table, then paused, hands behind her back, and looked out of the window. 'I've just seen Mike. But I'd like to hear your version first, before I decide what to do next.'

'We can explain everything!' Tracy leapt in.

Jo's eyebrows shot up and creased her clear forehead. 'I certainly hope so. I want you to tell me what went wrong this afternoon, and then I'll make a decision.'

Tracy frowned, but Holly put out a hand, palm upwards. 'We didn't set off on our second run down the rapids at exactly the right time,' she confessed. 'We were about five minutes late, and we *did* realise the others would be worried about us.'

Jo nodded. 'So, what went wrong?'

Holly took a deep breath. The afternoon sunlight sent deep shadow into the room, but Jo's flame-coloured hair was caught in the light. 'Nothing,' she said quietly.

'So, if nothing went wrong, what kept you?' She waited, but none of the three would answer. 'You say you realised that the others would worry? A lot can go wrong in five minutes. People can drown!'

'We're sorry, we couldn't help it.' Belinda sounded troubled. 'We were as quick as we could be!'

'And you won't tell me what held you up?'

They shook their heads.

'And what about the other problem? Mike tells me your life-jacket wasn't securely fastened?' Jo turned to Tracy. 'That in itself is serious, you know.'

Tracy nodded helplessly.

Jo stared at them. 'Then of course, you spoiled the day for the others.' She sighed. 'As you know, Mike's very bothered about this. He even advises having you sent home early.'

Holly heard the words. She stared at the old oak floorboards.

Jo sighed. 'It's something I'll have to consider carefully.' She held up a hand to stem their protests. 'Listen, Mike's a good, experienced group leader, and I've never known him express himself so strongly before. I trust his opinion, even though you may think he's being a bit strict on this occasion. I have to admit he has a point.' She paused by the door. 'I've told Mike I'd let him have my decision after I'd talked to you and slept on the problem.'

Holly began to breathe again. Jo Thomas was certainly trying her best to be fair. Perhaps all they would need would be a few more hours to go back to the cave and slot together the final pieces of the puzzle. 'Thanks,' she whispered.

'Oh, don't thank me,' Jo countered. 'I haven't made up my mind yet! I want you to join in with Mike's abseiling session this evening, while I'm thinking about things. It's your last chance to show him what you're really capable of. It's up to you!'

Then she left. They were not about to be punished on the spot. Holly breathed a sigh of relief.

'Wasn't she great about it?' Tracy whispered. 'Of course that makes me feel even more lousy about not being able to tell her what's going on!'

'I know.' Belinda scratched her head and frowned. 'I mean, she's just given us this last chance and everything . . .'

'Which we'll have to use to go back to Daniel's cave,' Holly pointed out. 'And that'll mean going against what Jo has just said again. She wants us to go abseiling after tea!'

'She'll feel we've really let her down this time if we sneak off and try to meet up with Daniel,' Belinda said.

'*When* we sneak off!' Holly said. 'Listen, in the end, once we find out the full story, Jo will

understand why we had to do this, won't she?'
She too hesitated over letting Jo down.

Tracy nodded at last. 'It's something we've got
to do.'

'But this time we need to be a step ahead
to throw Mike off the track. Any ideas?' Holly
asked.

'We'll have to play him at his own game,' Tracy
answered. 'If Mike's so good at setting Daniel
Martyn up to make it look as if he died in the
fall, we have to think of a foolproof way of setting
him up so we can slip away to meet Daniel.'

'Or one of us has to,' Belinda agreed. 'I mean,
if one or two of us could get away, that would do,
wouldn't it?' Her eyes lit up behind her glasses
and her voice lifted. 'Gather round. I think I have
a plan!'

Belinda dangled in mid-air. She hung from a sturdy
blue rope, safe inside a harness, but feeling the
entire universe tilt and turn. The red setting sun
swung crazily into view round the edge of the cliff,
the earth spun. At that moment, Belinda regretted
having volunteered her plan. *I must be mad!* she
thought. *I hate heights!* Then she remembered what
she had to do next. 'Help!' she cried out. 'I'm stuck!
I can't move!'

127

'For goodness sake, Belinda, stop fooling around!' Mike Sandford yelled from down below. 'Just do as I said!'

Belinda wailed. 'I can't remember what to do next! Somebody please help me!' She heard Mike's irritation and grinned to herself.

'Can't she do anything right?' he asked Tracy, who stood nearby at the foot of the cliff.

'I knew she should never have tried abseiling!' Tracy gasped. 'She can't stand heights! But she wouldn't listen; she really wanted to try it!' They looked up at Belinda swinging in mid-air. 'I think she really is in trouble, Mike!'

The plan had worked perfectly so far. Six of them – Holly, Tracy, Belinda, Steffie, Ollie and Mark – had gone with Mike up a quiet stretch of Butterpike Fell. They stopped when they came to the sheer cliff used by the centre for abseiling. Using a side path, they reached the top of the cliff, then strapped themselves into harnesses attached to ropes tethered to the rock. Mike had instructed them, then demonstrated the descent. Tracy, the first down after him, had eased herself over the cliff, swinging nimbly, finding footholds, lowering herself some thirty metres to the ground. It was then that she'd unharnessed herself and stood beside Mike to wait for Belinda. And now,

Belinda was spectacularly stuck! This was perfect. It would get Mike caught up in rescuing Belinda, while Holly and Tracy seized the chance to sneak off to High Force.

'What shall we do?' Tracy asked Mike now. 'Do you think you should climb up and rescue her?'

Mike clenched his teeth. 'It doesn't look as if there's any option!' He looked up at Belinda, still dangling, still claiming to be stuck.

Holly waited at the top of the cliff with the rest of the group. She peered anxiously over the edge. Belinda was putting in a brilliant performance.

Belinda met Holly's gaze as she hung there, seemingly limp and helpless. She gave her a quick grin and a wink. 'Oh help!' she cried. 'What am I supposed to do now?'

'Stay where you are!' Mike yelled at Holly's group. He turned to Tracy. 'That goes for you too. No one move until I get her down, OK?'

He set foot on the rock, then turned to Tracy with a frown. 'On second thoughts, you can climb alongside me and try to talk some sense into your friend.'

Tracy hesitated. This wasn't quite the way they'd planned it. 'OK!' she yelled back, taking a deep breath. If she disobeyed him now, he might get suspicious and the whole plan would collapse. 'Coming!' she called.

She scrambled up the first stretch of rock, already some ten metres behind Mike. 'Hang on and keep calm!' she told Belinda. 'We're on our way!' *Go on, Holly!* she thought. *You're on your own. It's now or never!*

Holly took it all in, then eased herself back from the edge of the cliff. She stared hard at Steffie and the two boys as she began to unfasten her harness and take off her helmet. 'Don't say anything!' she whispered.

'Oh no,' Steffie closed her eyes and groaned. 'Don't tell me!'

'What's she up to now?' Mark asked.

'Please!' Holly was desperate to get away before Mike noticed.

Suddenly Ollie stepped in. 'OK, we'll cover for you if we have to,' he said. He looked hard at Mark until he too nodded.

'Thanks!' Holly dropped her harness to the ground and looked to see if the coast was clear. High Force beckoned; she must reach it alone. There would be no back-up from Tracy if things went wrong at the cave.

She paused for a second longer. But it was now

or never; their very last chance to discover whether Daniel Martyn was still alive. Tomorrow would be too late. Holly set off for the wood, determined to give it her best shot.

11 *A shady deal*

The fellside drew down an evening mist as Holly
entered High Force. Silver-grey tree trunks soared
skywards and spread their leaves over her. Looking
back, she was sure no one could see her now.

She slowed to a jog, running easily down the hill,
until it cut away more steeply and she could hear
the roar of the waterfall below. At this moment, she
missed having Tracy and Belinda with her. They
would have decided things together and given
encouragement. But for the present she was on
her own. Thinking about it carefully, she decided
to head for the pool at the base of the fall. Then
she would climb up to the ledge and the hidden
cave as before.

She scrambled sideways down the slippery rocks,
keeping clear of the spray, clinging to roots and
branches to steady her descent. Wet ferns brushed
her bare arms and legs, a squirrel shot up a tree
trunk and sat chattering from a high branch.

Be there! Holly breathed, as she stood at last by the clear deep pool. She looked up at the thundering curtain of water, hoping that Daniel had read their brief message. 'WE WANT TO HELP' it read. Would he believe it? Would she find him there in the cave, waiting patiently for their return?

She climbed quickly up to the ledge. Maybe Mike had already discovered Belinda's trick that had let her slip away so neatly. No doubt he would set out to look for her. She hoped Belinda's and Tracy's nerve would hold. If they were forced to give in and tell where Holly had gone, she and Daniel would be in deep trouble.

She hauled herself on to the narrow ledge and paused to wipe the spray from her face and eyes.

'Daniel?' she called softly. 'Are you there?' She went down on to her hands and knees and crawled forward. 'Daniel, it's me, Holly Adams! We left a message. I need to talk to you!'

There was no reply. She inched behind the waterfall, crept inside the cave and began to look round warily. In the dim light, she could still make out their message in the sand. A careless footprint had rubbed out part of the words; a print with a deep indented pattern. It was a scuff mark from a walking boot. 'At least he's been here. He must have seen it!' Holly muttered to herself. 'But where is he now?' She took a torch from her back pocket and shone it into the gloom. 'Daniel?' she called again.

There was movement behind her. A tall, silent shape stood blocking the exit. She spun round with a sharp intake of breath and shone the torch. The light forced him to put up his hand to shade his eyes. She saw that one leg of his jeans was ripped, and a strip of denim cloth tied round his wrist. She let out a cry of surprise.

'I was waiting. I watched you come in,' he said calmly. He stooped and crept forward into the cave. 'Who are you and what do you want?'

Holly sensed the tension. She realised the reason. All Daniel knew was that she was the same girl who'd first set up the alarm when he jumped from the car. Why should he trust her, after she'd done that to him? She swung the torch away and waited for him to advance. Danger seemed to hang in the air as he came closer.

'What do you want?' The boy's dark eyes gleamed. He squatted a metre or so away, wary and hostile. 'Why can't you keep your nose out of things?'

'I know how it must seem!' she began. She felt

her heart thump. How did she know for sure that all their theories about him were right? That Mike hated him for some reason of his own, and wanted rid of him? What if she and Tracy and Belinda had been wrong from the very start?

Holly stared warily back at him, then found her voice at last. 'We *do* want to help!' she insisted. 'But we need to understand what's going on. What has Mike Sandford got against you? What's his link with those two other men, Slingsby and Carter?'

Daniel shrugged and pushed the long, dark hair from his face. 'What's it to you? Why don't you just stay out of it?' He edged back against the wall of the cave, then sat down, one leg crooked, one outstretched.

Holly had time to study him closely. His face was thin, and in the shadowy cave, in the strange, liquid light cast by the waterfall, his dark eyes looked huge. His brows were flat and widely spaced, his nose long and thin. The denim shirt he wore had a strip torn away from the bottom hem. His jeans were torn at both knees, as well as ripped at the bottom. He wore a pair of sturdy walking boots.

'I think Mike Sandford is planning to kill you!' she whispered. She must win his confidence, and do it quickly. She told him about Tracy and Belinda and the threats they'd overheard in the garden at the Cross Keys. 'He means business!' she insisted. 'And now he wants to get rid of us too!'

She described how Mike had disliked them all along for interfering, how they suspected that he'd found their notebook full of their notes and suspicions. 'He warned the head of the activity centre about us. After tonight, we're bound to get sent home. This is our last chance to put things right!' she pleaded.

Daniel knitted his brows. He ran his free hand through the sand. 'Don't mess with Mike,' he warned. 'You don't know what you're getting into.'

'It's too late! We're already in!' Holly edged towards him. 'And I want you to tell me what he's up to. Then maybe we could help put a stop to it, whatever it is!'

'We?' Daniel clung to his puzzled, suspicious expression.

'The three of us; me, Belinda and Tracy. After all, we're the three who made a mess of your getaway from the car.'

He sighed. 'Don't think I don't know it!'

'Sorry!' Holly was desperate to shake information

out of him, but she knew she must go slowly. She felt that gradually she was gaining Daniel's trust. 'How did you get mixed up with Mike Sandford yourself?' she persisted.

'We met up in Africa,' Daniel said. Each word was mumbled, indistinct through the roar of the waterfall.

Holly nodded. 'That's where he had his last job?'

'Kenya. I was on safari with my folks. In Mike's group. We all thought he was a good guy.'

'So did we,' Holly agreed. 'That's how he comes across at first.' Relaxed, unflappable, a regular nice guy. 'So what happened?'

'My parents had to stay on after the holiday. They work in wildlife conservation and they had some business to finish. I had to come back to England for school.' Daniel shook his head and let a wry grin escape. 'Since Mike was travelling straight back here, and since they thought he was genuine, they asked if I could come back with him, and stay with him in the Lakes for a couple of weeks, before school started.'

'And Mike agreed?'

He nodded. 'They paid him some money. Anyway, he must have realised I'd make a good cover.'

'For what?' Holly had edged still closer to Daniel. 'Cover for what? What's he up to?'

Daniel gave a short laugh. 'You'd never guess!'

'Diamonds!' she said promptly. 'We think it might have something to do with diamonds.'

He opened his eyes wide. 'Pretty smart. How did you figure that out?'

Holly explained the Amsterdam link. 'We know Slingsby and Carter had dropped the rough stones off there to have them polished. And now they've gone back to collect them,' she told him. 'Only we couldn't work out why it had to be undercover. And it still isn't clear why Mike turned against you!'

'What if I told you they were stolen?' Daniel said. The rush of water almost drowned out his voice.

'Mike stole the diamonds?' she repeated.

Daniel shrugged. 'Well, there's no way he could afford to buy them, is there? Not on his salary!'

'How? How did he steal them?'

'Who knows? When I came to think about it later, there were meetings during our safari; people he met up with on the quiet. There was plenty of chance to do a deal over some dodgy diamonds. I'm not saying he stole them himself, don't get me wrong. But he knew they were stolen; a whole leather pouch full of uncut stones. I think he's a fence for the actual gang of thieves. You know, a kind of middleman.'

'How did you find all this out?'

'Easy.' Daniel stabbed at the sand with his finger. 'He dumped them on me to get through Customs. He wasn't going to take the risk of smuggling them through himself, was he? Only, he never expected me to find them either. He'd cut a neat slit in the bottom of my rucksack, see? He made a false compartment, shoved the stones in, sealed it with tape. Customs never even bothered to search me. I guess I looked respectable then!' He laughed again.

'Anyway, there I was sitting waiting for him in the Arrivals lounge. Mike was coming through Customs after me. They searched him! I'm waiting, and I notice this little taped-up slit near the bottom of my bag. I'm pulling the tape off, looking inside it, taking out the pouch full of what looks like junky little bits of rough glass, when Mike runs up and grabs them from me. That's when it clicked. He'd tricked me into bringing stolen diamonds through Customs for him!'

Daniel paused for breath. 'Before I have a chance to think, and I'm pretty slow to react because of the shock, Mike bundles me into a hire car and drives like a maniac up the motorway to the Lakes, non-stop. Next thing I know, he's on the mobile phone to a guy called Carter.'

'Tony Carter!' Holly nodded. 'I knew he fitted in somewhere. Slingsby as well?'

'Yes, they're both in on it. They're the ones with the contacts in Holland. Mike went to college with Slingsby. They go back a long way. They're genuine careworkers, but I guess Mike persuaded them to go in on this with him. Anyway, Mike calls Carter and tells him there's been a slip-up. "The kid poked his nose in," he says. "Come up with something, will you?" Then he fixes up a meeting with him in Kendal. He puts down the phone. I know it's going to be something nasty. I just have to sit in the car and wait!'

'Another set-up?' Holly asked.

'Yep. He meets Carter. They talk, but I can't hear. We drive on for a bit. I'm bundled out of the car, up a driveway into a big house. Later, I find out it belongs to a friend of Carter's who's abroad on holiday. It's way out of town, in the middle of nowhere, it's the middle of the night, the window's busted in. Slingsby and Carter have made it look like a break-in, then they've made a quick getaway. Mike gets me in there at knife-point, the cop sirens are already screaming. At the last second, Mike makes a run for it and jumps in the car. He's off.

I'm left running down the drive, looking like I've broken into the stupid house. Caught red-handed, you might say.'

'So they arrested you?' Holly bit her lip. Daniel had had things really rough. 'Didn't they contact your parents?'

He shrugged. 'How? They were in central Africa somewhere. They have to travel in the bush; they're not on the end of a phone.'

'And you couldn't make the police listen to you?'

'Who can blame them? Here I was, some crazy kid going on about bringing stolen diamonds out of Africa. I told them I never broke into the lousy house. They said, pull the other one! Mike had sewn me up good and proper. I might as well have been still carrying the brick that bust the window! And no one was going to listen to a word I said!'

Holly nodded. 'And Mike knew you'd be put into care if they couldn't contact your mum and dad. They worked it so that Carter picked up your case? Wow!'

'That's about it!' Daniel drew breath and leaned his head back against the rock. 'There was only one problem as far as they were concerned. They didn't know I planned to do a runner. No way was I going

141

to sit back and let Mike and the other two get clear, diamonds and all! I knew I might be able to stop them if I could just get out of that crummy car. This was after I'd been locked up in a police station for a couple of nights, before Carter took charge of me and we were on our way down to Kendal, taking me to the detention centre near there.'

Holly sighed. 'And that was when we moved in?'

'Just my luck,' Daniel admitted. 'I never reckoned on anyone getting in the way when I jumped!' He gave a tight smile. 'And the rest, as they say, is history!'

'Not quite. There's just one bit that's still not clear. I get the plan about smuggling the diamonds, and the bit about framing you for a robbery you didn't do, so the police wouldn't believe your story about the jewels. But what about the fall from the cliff? Who was that, if it wasn't you crashing into the lake? Or did you come up to the surface and swim off?'

'Ah!' Daniel raised himself to his feet, nursing his hand. He turned to face Holly. 'Don't you get it?'

'No. We just saw a body. The other three came walking back down the hill. You didn't. Naturally we thought—'

142

'You *thought* you saw a body!' Daniel cut in. 'Everyone *thought* they saw someone hit the lake. That's how it was meant to look!'

'You mean . . .!' Had Holly heard this right? Was he saying there was no body after all?

'Did they ever find anything in the water?' he asked.

'No.' The police had dragged the lake for hours. They'd put out appeals for information. 'Nothing. Nobody.'

'That's because there was nobody. *No body*. Get it?' Daniel paused for a moment. 'Look, I'm climbing my way out of trouble, but Slingsby manages to cut me off. Mike throws his knife up to him. Slingsby gets me against the cliff, lashes out at my arm. I have to wrestle the knife off him.' He went to the ledge and showed Holly the heavy black scouting knife which they'd discovered on their first visit to the cave. Then he pointed to his injured wrist.

Holly remembered the shouted cries, the invisible fight.

'I give as good as I get. I grab the knife and make a getaway. What are they going to do about this now? I'm climbing the rocks the best I can, when I hear Mike yell at Carter to take his jacket off. Mike pulls out a spare waterproof outfit; a kagoul and a pair of trousers from his own backpack and I turn just in time to see them unrolling the things, and shoving heather and rocks inside the clothes. They stuff the arms and legs and the hood.'

'Like a scarecrow?' Holly got the picture. 'You mean, that's what they threw off the cliff?' In her memory, she saw the blurred shape falling, crashing down into the depths of the lake. 'Just a bundle of clothes and rocks?' She breathed a deep sigh of relief, then laughed.

Daniel gave her time for it to sink in. 'It was a decoy, to throw you all off the trail. Mike saw I was getting away, but he thought he could deal with me later. He knew I wouldn't get far, not with this gash on my arm. It bled pretty badly at first.'

'No wonder they never found anything in the lake!' Holly said. 'That bundle of stuff would sink right to the bottom!' She remembered too that Carter had come back down the hillside without his jacket. Every detail fitted in with Daniel's account. 'And if and when he did catch up with you, he'd be able to finish the thing properly. He'd get rid of you for good?' Her voice sounded hollow in the dark cave. She walked angrily towards the exit.

'Yeah, he had it in for me. I knew that.'

144

'An invisible murder!' she exclaimed. 'If the police thought you'd drowned in the lake, how could Mike possibly kill someone who was already dead? Who would even go looking for a body? Who would ever know?' The daring and cleverness of Mike's scheme took her breath away.

'Right!' Daniel nodded. Only, he hasn't got me yet! I've kept one step ahead. So far!'

'But you *were* at Rover's Cottage the night Belinda got lost?'

He gave a small nod. 'Yeah. Say thanks to her from me, will you? If she hadn't come barging in through the window like that, I might have stayed asleep upstairs when Mike came looking for me. As it was, she woke me up and I got out quick. She most likely saved my life!'

Holly smiled. 'She'll be glad about that.' Then she grew serious again. 'Why did you hide in the cottage when you knew Mike was still after you?'

Daniel pointed to his bandaged wrist. 'For a start, I couldn't get far with this. It hurt a lot. I felt pretty weak as well, from the blood I'd lost. Anyway, like I said, Mike had set me up to look like a thief. I had to stick around to clear my name.'

'And I expect he *knew* you wouldn't get far, so he came up on to the fell later that night. Rover's Cottage would be just one of the places he wanted to search.' Holly worked it all out at last. 'I remember Mike was pretty mad when he got there and found us instead of you. We couldn't understand what had got into him!'

'Murder!' Daniel reminded her. 'That's what. That and the diamonds.'

Holly saw Mike in the full glare of his anger. He'd stormed at them, then covered his tracks and tried to get rid of them for interfering and getting in his way. It all made sense.

And now she trembled for Daniel. Mike would never give in, it seemed. Tomorrow the diamonds would be safe in his hands, cut and polished to perfection. And, if Mike got his way, Daniel wouldn't be alive to tell the tale. 'You're in terrible danger!' She spoke into the roar and rush of the waterfall. 'Thank heavens you believed our message!' She pointed to the scuffed words in the sand. 'Thank heavens you stuck around to tell me what's really going on!' She met his dark gaze with a smile.

Daniel nodded twice.

'Now what we need is another plan to beat Mike at his own game. Something that shows him up for what he really is.'

'Are you sure?' Daniel looked up at the rough, damp arch of rock that formed the roof of the cave. 'I said you'd better not mess with Mike, remember?'

'Yes, and I said it was too late. We're in this together, OK?'

He smiled and nodded. 'So what's the plan?'

12 To catch a thief

Tracy talked quietly to Belinda to guide her down the cliff face. 'That's right, put your left foot on that ledge. Let the rope take your weight. You're quite safe. Good!'

'Listen, you're strapped in; you can't possibly fall.' Mike Sandford had scaled the cliff to reach Belinda. He seemed to be trying to hide his irritation from the group up above.

'Shh. You'll only make her more nervous!' Tracy advised. She made eye contact with Belinda. Things were going well. By now, Holly should have reached High Force. 'OK, now swing out from the ledge and lower yourself gradually. That's good. Now, push off with both feet! Great!' Tracy eased Belinda down to ground level, taking her time, giving Holly the best chance she could to get away.

Mike jumped on to the ground. He stood watching as Tracy offered Belinda a hand down the last metre or so. 'I might have known, things can never be simple with you lot,' he said.

Belinda grinned at Tracy. 'You know something? I think I just got over my vertigo! Hanging there in mid-air, I had time to take in the scenery and to stop feeling dizzy and sick. I think I'm cured for good!' She loosened her harness and stepped clear.

Tracy grinned back, proud of the way Belinda had volunteered for the trick despite her real fear of heights. 'That's great!'

But Mike was frowning up at the cliff. 'OK, Holly, your turn!' he shouted. There was no reply. He yelled again. 'Steffie, tell Holly to get a move on, will you? She should be on her way down by now!' He cupped his hands round his mouth. 'Holly! Steffie! Stop messing about up there and get started. We can't wait all night!'

Ollie's face peered over the ledge instead. 'Can I come down next?' he shouted.

'No, I want Holly down here before you. Send her down, please!' He waited as Ollie withdrew reluctantly out of sight.

After a few more seconds, Steffie's face appeared. 'Holly's not that keen, Mike. Will I do?'

Mike peered up at the cliff top. 'What's going on up there?'

149

'Nothing!' Steffie stared back, looking innocent.
'Why, you little . . .!' Mike realised he'd been tricked. 'She's not there, is she?' Seizing a dangling rope, he flung it furiously against the rock. Then he made a grab for Tracy. 'You did this on purpose, didn't you?' He swung her off her feet. She stumbled, regained her balance and backed away out of reach. 'I suppose you think you're pretty smart!'

Suddenly he spun round and went for Belinda instead. She ducked and jumped sideways. He crouched, ready to rush at them again, cornering them against the cliff face. 'You set me up so your friend could sneak off!'

'I don't know what you're talking about,' Belinda said. They watched his every move; the flicking muscle in his eyelid, the staring brown eyes.

'Tell me where she's gone!' he snarled.

Belinda stared back defiantly as he moved in on her. She was scared, but she would never give in.

Then something seemed to click in his thoughts. He stood upright, unexpectedly calm. 'Got it!' he said, as if he'd solved a difficult puzzle. 'High Force!'

Tracy couldn't hide a gasp of surprise. It told him that he'd guessed right.

'The waterfall; that's the spot, isn't it? Why didn't I think of that earlier?'

150

'I don't know what you mean,' Belinda said steadily. But she knew she could only delay things for a few more seconds.

'Don't you?' He backed off, watching them like a hawk. 'When you were late bringing your raft down, I knew you were up to something. But I couldn't figure it out. Now I can.' He stopped short, as if he'd been about to say too much.

Scared as she was, Tracy challenged him. 'Why? What could we be up to? Who do you think held us up?' She wanted to get him to confess that he knew Daniel Martyn was still alive.

Mike took another step towards them, his eyes narrowed. 'You're crazy!' he retorted. Then he swung away again, without waiting to talk himself out of the corner he'd been getting himself into. He turned away from the cliff and set off across country towards High Force.

Belinda looked at Tracy. 'He knows we know!' she gasped. 'That's for sure.'

'About Daniel being alive?'

'Yes; you could see it in his face.'

Tracy nodded. 'But we can't just let him go!' He'd thought too quickly for them to stop him from giving chase.

Belinda agreed. 'We can't stop him, it's too late for that. But we can go after him. Come on!' They

151

began to sprint, twenty metres or so behind Mike Sandford as he headed for the waterfall.

'Maybe he won't find the cave!' Tracy gasped. She leapt over rocks partly hidden by the ferns.

Belinda nodded. 'It's well hidden. Let's just hope Daniel and Holly stay in there until the coast's clear!'

Mike was gaining on them, running strongly over the rough ground. They stumbled as they ran, desperate to keep him in their sights.

Holly had thought of a plan, and it was a daring one. If the diamonds were worth a fortune, then Mike would go to any lengths to keep them. They knew that already. 'What we have to do is get hold of them before he does!' she told Daniel earnestly. 'Mike's arranged to pick them up tomorrow. But we have to stop him.'

He narrowed his eyes and went to crouch by the entrance to the cave. His old, suspicious look had returned. 'You make it sound dead easy.'

Holly could understand his doubts. 'Oh, no, it'll be hard, don't get me wrong. It'll need perfect timing!' She was thinking. 'But listen; Slingsby and Carter are meeting up with Mike at twelve tomorrow. They'll bring the diamonds.'

He nodded. 'So?'

'They'll be expecting Mike.'

'Yes.'

'So somehow we've got to get there before him!'

'And?' Daniel flicked open the blade of the heavy scouting knife. He frowned as he listened and scored deep marks in the sand.

'And we'll steal the diamonds back ourselves!' she announced.

'Just like that?' He dug the blade in the ground and turned away.

'No, listen! Slingsby and Carter won't be expecting us. We'll have to make sure they don't recognise us, OK? Just keep it clear; what we have to do is steal the diamonds before Mike gets there, OK!'

'Supposing we can,' Daniel asked. 'What would be the point?'

'Set a thief to catch a thief!' Holly explained. Her idea swept her along; she felt sure it could work. 'Did you ever hear that saying?'

'Sure, but tell me straight, will you? I still don't get it!'

'OK, *we're* the thieves now. We snatch the loot from the real villains. And there's the evidence you need. You go straight to the police, dump the diamonds on their desk and tell them the whole story! Then they'll have to believe you!'

Daniel was still hunched by the narrow ledge. He thought long and hard. 'It could work,' he agreed. 'With the diamonds as proof!'

'It *has* to work!' She had to convince him to give it a try. 'Unless you can come up with something else?'

He shook his head and sighed. 'Just hold on. We get there before Mike. We steal the stones. We make a quick getaway before Mike has a chance to stop us. Is that it?'

Holly nodded and waited with held breath for him to decide.

'OK, it's worth a try!' he said at last.

She grinned. 'Great! So, you meet us in Windermere tomorrow morning at eleven forty-five. By the steamboat jetty.' She made firm plans, rushing to set things up so she could get back and help out Tracy and Belinda, who were bound to be in trouble with Mike by now.

'How will you three get there?' he asked.

She shrugged. 'My guess is, we'll be on the first bus out of Butterpike village tomorrow morning, after all that's happened today. Anyway, nothing will stop us being there now.' She looked him in the eyes and smiled. 'We'll make it all right.'

He grinned back at her. 'I believe you,' he said. 'Don't ask me why, but I do!' He shoved his dark hair back. 'And thanks!'

'Don't thank us yet,' she cut in. 'Save that for when it's all over!'

He nodded, then made way for Holly to crawl past him on to the ledge. She felt fresh spray on her bare skin.

'Good hiding-place!' She paused to congratulate him.

'Yeah!'

For the first time, Holly saw the frown truly disappear from Daniel's face. His eyes lightened up.

He smiled. 'And thanks, anyway!' he said, ducking his head sideways. 'For doing all this for me!'

She blushed. 'That's OK. Now all you have to do is stay out of Mike's way for one more night!'

He laughed. 'I'll do my best!'

'And meet us in Windermere just before midday tomorrow!' She crawled out into the open air, leaving Daniel sitting safe inside his cave.

Holly eased her way along the ledge, then glanced up to judge the distance to the top of the waterfall. It would be the quickest way out of the woods. She set her mind to it and began the slippery climb.

She had her fingertips on the top ridge and was just hauling herself up the last metre when she heard shouts. She pulled herself up to glimpse Mike Sandford charging through the trees towards her, with Belinda and Tracy not far behind.

'Holly, watch out!' Belinda yelled. 'He's on to you!'

Still she clung by her fingertips to the slippery rocks, beside the gushing waterfall. It took a split second to work things out. Now Mike was smashing his way through ferns and bushes to reach her. Tracy and Belinda came flying after him.

Holly glanced back down to the ledge that led to the cave. Good; Daniel had had the sense to stay hidden. But she had Mike Sandford to deal with; his threats, his questions. Quickly she heaved herself up, lay flat on her stomach and rolled away from the dangerous edge. But before she could get to her feet, Mike came splashing through the stream that fed the waterfall, wading through the water, to seize her by the arm. She staggered and fell.

Mike dragged her to her feet, then overbalanced back into the stream. They were both soaking wet.

Belinda and Tracy were still scrambling down through the wood towards them. But they stopped short when they saw Holly held fast in Mike's grasp. Holly and Mike were close to the edge of the waterfall. The stream whirled around their legs. He seemed to be trying to push her over!

With a huge effort, Holly twisted sideways. Mike lost his footing and stumbled on the moss-covered rocks. He let go. She waded deeper into the stream. Swearing, he turned round to follow her.

'You won't get away with this, you hear!' he yelled above the water's roar. Again he lurched towards her.

She was cut off from Belinda and Tracy, backing towards the edge. She half fell, but she broke her fall with her outstretched arms. She slid sideways to avoid Mike's lurching figure. Close to the edge; too close. The water slid in a massive, gleaming stream, then fell away into white spray, down into the deep pool below.

Mike lunged yet again. Holly ducked. The current pulled at her. She tried to grab at tree roots, missed, and slid nearer to the edge.

'Holly!' Tracy shouted a desperate warning.

She tried to stop herself and scrambled to her knees, half blinded by spray. Mike was bound to try again. He wanted her over the edge. She could see the look in his eyes. But before he had time to reach out and push, she twisted on to her feet, poised, ready to jump. Then she sprang into mid-air, hidden by rising spray, falling, falling!

She landed cleanly in the cold, clear water. Down she went, feet first, bubbles rising, her shirt ballooning round her shoulders. Then she hit the bottom and launched herself back up. She opened her eyes, turned her face upwards, and rose towards the bright, greeny-blue light of the surface.

'Holly!' Belinda screamed as she saw her vanish, and blew her emergency whistle for help. She and Tracy rushed to the water's edge, past Mike, who had caught hold of a branch to stop himself from falling after Holly. They peered down into the pool.

Tracy took one horrified look. The surface of the pool bubbled and swirled. But there was no sign of Holly.

'She's gone!' Belinda gasped. 'She must have fallen against a rock and hit her head. Tracy, I think Holly's drowning!'

There was no time to stop and consider. Tracy drew a deep breath. 'Ready?' she asked.

Belinda took off her glasses and nodded.

'Let's go!' Tracy took a tremendous leap through the air, followed by Belinda. They plummeted down. They would rescue Holly. They would risk anything to save her.

Two more figures plunged into the crystal depths. One head bobbed to the surface, its brown hair drifting free behind. Holly gasped for air. Way above, Mike Sandford was a tiny head-and-shoulders figure peering helplessly down. Soon, Tracy's fair head rose to meet her, her strong limbs swimming across the pool.

'Are you OK?'

'Yes, no problem. See!' Holly swam a few strokes. 'Where's Belinda?'

'Here!' Belinda had bobbed to the surface alongside them. 'Is everyone OK?'

'Yes, you can cut your life-saving routine!' Tracy said, laughing with relief. 'It looks like Holly jumped of her own free will!'

Belinda blinked and pushed her hair from her face. 'Typical! We're supposed to be trying to save you, you idiot!' Figures were running through the woods in response to Belinda's alarm.

'Thanks anyway!' Holly swam towards a part of the bank which sloped gently into the water. By the time they reached the shingly beach, the rescuers had arrived.

They glanced up to see where Mike had got to. He'd seen the group come running from the

Hall and begun to climb down the side of the waterfall. They heard him call to Jo Thomas. He came straight past the ledge leading to Daniel's cave without suspecting a thing. Holly breathed another sigh of relief.

'What now?' Jo demanded. 'First, is everyone OK?' She surveyed the three dripping figures, then turned to Mike for an explanation.

He drew sharp, angry breaths. 'I've had it up to here with these three!' he shouted. 'Enough is enough! Either they go, or I do!'

Jo listened to his version of events; how Belinda had deliberately tricked him on the abseiling route, how Holly had slipped off on some secret assignation. 'And then these three lunatics all jump from the top of the fall!' he yelled. 'Are they crazy, or something?'

Holly stood listening calmly. 'Belinda and Tracy thought I was drowning,' she explained. But there seemed little point in arguing. In fact, now that she had a plan for tomorrow, it would be better to get thrown off the course. She narrowed her eyes at Tracy and Belinda, warning them to stay quiet. They waited for Jo's decision.

Jo folded her arms and sighed. 'This time you've gone too far,' she said quietly. 'I gave you one last chance and it seems you messed it up completely.

160

All this fooling around is dangerous, as you very well know!'

Holly stood in her dripping clothes. They felt suddenly clammy and cold. She heard Jo's words through a daze. It was what she wanted, but it hurt her pride all the same.

'I've no alternative. I can't take responsibility for keeping you at Butterpike Hall any longer. I'll have to send you home.'

Mike nodded; a single, grim tilt of his head. Belinda and Tracy shifted uneasily at her side. Holly stood firm. She said nothing.

Jo continued. 'You three will pack your bags this evening. Meanwhile, I'll phone your headmistress and suggest that I drive you to Windermere tomorrow morning, where she can collect you and take you back to Willow Dale.' She paused, grim-faced. 'I can't imagine she'll be too pleased with you when she hears what's been going on.'

Tracy sighed. Belinda hung her head. Holly stood rigid, meeting Jo's gaze.

'You understand what I'm telling you?' she insisted. 'I'm throwing all three of you off the course!' She turned on her heel, leaving them to their shared disgrace.

Behind them Mike gave a satisfied grunt, then

trooped off at the head of the rescue party, back towards the Hall.

Holly waited until they were out of hearing. 'Yes!' she jumped up and punched the air in a victory salute. 'We've been thrown out at last!' She turned to Tracy and Belinda, her face wreathed in smiles.

'Hey!' Belinda said. 'I'm the one who's supposed to cheer when that happens. I've hated every minute, remember!' She grinned widely.

'No, no, you've loved it. It's been *fun!*' Tracy was wringing out her shirt. 'I for one am really cut up about it!' But she too was grinning from ear to ear. 'So what's the plan now? Come on, Holly, fill us in!'

Holly linked arms with them and set off towards the Hall. Their feet squelched over the heather, their clothes still dripped. 'Well,' she began. 'How do you two fancy turning diamond thieves for the day?' And she started to explain the plan to save Daniel Martyn.

13 Desperate remedies

Steffie hovered in the girls' dormitory by Tracy's bed. 'I'm really sorry,' she told them.

Tracy went on packing her rucksack. She planned what to keep to one side to wear next day; T-shirt, jeans, trainers. She shook her head. 'Thanks, Steffie. But no need to worry about us.'

Steffie sighed. 'Yes, but they've thrown you off the course!' She sat on Tracy's bed, leaning back on both arms.

Holly stopped packing and turned to Steffie. 'Listen, it really isn't as bad as it looks.' She had to stop herself from seeming too happy about the way things had turned out.

'Is that so?' Steffie only sounded more curious. 'I never know with you three; you're always full of surprises. There's obviously something going on!'

'No, really!' Tracy took her hairbrush from the drawer and put it into her bag. She gave Steffie a sweet look.

'Yes, really!' Steffie grinned. 'Look, why not let me in on this?' She turned to Belinda. 'Why are they so happy to be leaving? It doesn't make sense.'

Belinda shook her head. 'You've got it all wrong, Steffie. We're very upset. I mean, think about it; what's Miss Horswell going to say? Come to that, what's my mum going to say?' She sighed as she took a frilly white blouse and smart skirt from her locker, clothes which Mrs Hayes had insisted that Belinda bring with her. 'She's going to be awfully upset with me now!'

'"Oh, Belinda, how could you?"' Tracy mimicked Mrs Hayes's fussy manner. She seized Belinda's crisp new blouse and held it up against her. '"And you never even wore this lovely blouse I bought specially for you!"'

'Lay off, Tracy,' Belinda muttered. She snatched at the blouse. 'God, mothers are so embarrassing!' She began to stuff the unwanted shirt deep into her bag.

'No, hang on a minute!' Holly reached out to grab the blouse. Belinda had crumpled it up, so she turned to Steffie. 'If you really want to do something useful . . .' she began.

'I do!' Steffie jumped up, ready for action.

'. . . You could dash along to the linen room,

where they keep the iron, and run it over this,' she finished, holding out Belinda's blouse.

'Oh.' Steffie's face fell.

Tracy laughed. 'Yes, go ahead, Steffie, leave us to pack in peace. Can't you see how this disgrace is getting to us!' She put a hand to her brow in tragic-heroine pose.

Steffie wrinkled her nose, then grabbed the blouse. 'Oh, OK, then. I can see when I'm not wanted!' She gave up and breezed out of the dormitory. 'You really want me to iron this?' she asked.

Holly nodded. 'Yes, please. Belinda's wearing it to go home in tomorrow.'

Steffie couldn't hide her grin as she waved and pulled the door to after her.

'I am?' Belinda stood, hands on hips. 'Holly, have you taken a proper look at that blouse? It's got . . . frills!'

'Exactly.' Holly enjoyed Belinda's dismay. 'It's nice and smart. Isn't that how your mum would like you to look?'

Tracy broke in. 'Come on, Holly, what are you up to now? It's not really for Belinda's mum, all this business with the shirt, is it?'

Holly grinned and sat on her bed. ''Course not. But it is smart, you have to admit. And so is that skirt.'

'So?' Belinda felt another of Holly's ideas creeping up on her. 'You're not expecting me to wear those things?'

'They're just what I had in mind for tomorrow. Thank heavens for your mum, Belinda; otherwise we'd have been really stuck.'

Belinda and Tracy stared at each other. 'OK, Holly Adams!' Tracy launched herself on to Holly's bed and lay flat on her back, arms behind her head. 'I'm not going to move from this bed until you've told us what you mean.'

'And I'm not wearing that horrible blouse unless you give me a very good reason!' Belinda followed suit, flopping on to the bed with her head next to Tracy's feet.

Holly laughed out loud. 'OK, the skirt and blouse are what the well-dressed thief is wearing!' The final part of the plan had come to her when she spotted Belinda trying to stuff them into her bag.

'Thief?' Belinda echoed.

Holly nodded and rushed into her explanation. 'OK, I'm not kidding now. We're going to steal the diamonds back from Mike! Daniel has agreed to do it with us. I said I'd work everything out with you before we meet up at the Coffee Pot tomorrow. I've been planning it ever since I left the cave, but I admit I was pretty stuck on that particular point.'

166

Tracy nodded and propped herself on her elbows. 'Like, how do we steal a bag of diamonds from three fully grown men?'

'We could try to split them up, Belinda suggested. She sounded calm and matter of fact. 'If we can separate Mike, Slingsby and Carter, they would be easier to deal with one by one.'

Holly nodded. 'That's what I thought. And that's where your blouse and skirt come in!'

Belinda backed off under her gaze. 'Why do I feel sure I'm not going to like this?' she protested.

Tracy grabbed the tailored black skirt and held it up against Belinda. 'Cinderella, you *shall* go to the ball!' she laughed. 'But seriously, Holly, why does Belinda have to get dressed up in these things?'

Holly cleared her throat. 'She's going to be a waitress!'

'I am?' Belinda blinked at Holly from behind her glasses.

'You are! You're going to be the new waitress at the Coffee Pot.' Holly sounded quite definite.

'Does the cafe owner know about this?' Tracy grinned. She liked the idea of Belinda in disguise.

'Not yet,' Holly admitted. 'That's where *we* come in.' She explained to Tracy how they would have to distract the cafe owner's attention while Belinda slipped in to wait on Slingsby and Carter's table.

167

'They'll be there first, waiting for Mike. They'll have the diamonds with them.'

'What do I say to them?' Panic had begun to show on Belinda's face. 'What if they recognise me from earlier in the week?'

But Tracy had entered into the spirit of things, and wouldn't hear a word said against Holly's plan. 'They won't! Not if you take off your glasses and put your hair up. You'll look completely different! You'll look great!' she reassured her.

'But what do I say?'

Holly paused and frowned. 'Let's see. We still need something to get them apart somehow. I've got it. You have to bring a message for one of them! Something about the phone . . . that's it! You come up to the table and tell Mr Carter that there's an urgent phone message from a Mr Mike Sandford!'

'Great!' Tracy nodded. 'He'll fall for that for sure!'

'So he rushes off to answer a phone call that doesn't exist, and Tracy, Daniel and I will be waiting for him,' Holly explained.

'We jump him!' Tracy agreed. 'We'll grab the diamonds and run for it!'

'Easier said than done,' Belinda warned. But she was beginning to see the possibilities of the plan.

'Just one other thing.' Tracy looked thoughtful. 'We're assuming it'll be Carter who has the diamonds on him. But what if it's Slingsby?'

Holly frowned. 'No, listen. Carter's been in charge of that side of things. I think we can bank on him keeping hold of the diamonds until he hands them over to Mike. What do you think?'

Belinda and Tracy nodded.

Holly took a deep breath. 'Do you think it'll work?'

They all looked at one another wide-eyed, serious. Slowly they nodded.

'Desperate situations need desperate remedies,' Belinda said.

'With good timing and a bit of good luck,' Tracy agreed. 'I think it's a great plan. Well done, Holly!'

Belinda thought of another possible snag. 'What if Mike gets to the cafe before us? That would ruin everything!'

But Tracy jumped in. 'He won't!' she cried.

'How do you know?' Holly asked.

'Because I heard him discussing us in Jo's office about ten minutes ago!' Tracy could hardly get out the words. Her blue eyes were fired up. 'Jo was saying she'd spoken to Miss Horswell and they'd agreed on Windermere bus station as a good halfway point to drop us off tomorrow. That way Miss Horswell won't have so far to drive. She said to Mike she'd have to set off at about ten-thirty to get there in time. But Mike said he'd take us in the Land-rover instead. In fact, he insisted! And anyway, he said he had something he wanted to do while he was in town!'

'You can say that again!' Belinda said dryly. 'Just the little matter of a bag full of diamonds to pick up!'

'And what did Jo say?' Holly asked.

'She said OK. He said he'd drop us off in Windermere bus station just after eleven-thirty.'

Holly smiled. 'So we'll know exactly where he is, and we won't have to worry about him getting to the cafe before us!' There was still lots to think about, but it felt good to be organising and planning their way through. 'We'd better try and get an early night,' she said, glancing out of the window at the gathering dusk.

Tracy nodded. 'I'll go along and see if Steffie has finished ironing that shirt.' She laughed as she opened the door. 'Belinda as a waitress!' she said with a glint of mischief in her eyes. 'Now, this I have to see!'

'And I'll go down and pick up a street map of Windermere from the rack in the games room,'

170

Belinda told Holly. 'We might well need one tomorrow!'

'Good thinking.' Holly went back to her packing with a mixture of fear and excitement. They had a plan. It was a good one. Mike wouldn't suspect a thing as he drove them off in disgrace. He'd be driving straight into their trap!

But when the three of them went to bed at ten o'clock, they stared through the window at the bright moon, unable to sleep. They thought of Daniel, in the cave behind the waterfall at High Force, constantly on the lookout for Mike Sandford. He would have to spend the night watching his own shadow.

Tomorrow they would meet him by Lake Windermere. But tonight, there was nothing they could do to help.

14 An urgent phone call

Next morning, Mike stared at Belinda, unable to hide the sneer on his face. 'You needn't think that dressing up nice and smart is going to impress anyone!' he told her.

She blushed and glanced down at her new white blouse and black skirt. She stood with Holly and Tracy, beside their rucksacks in the old entrance hall to Butterpike Hall. It was ten o'clock on Friday morning.

'Your headmistress is furious with you all.' Mike enjoyed watching their downcast faces. 'According to Jo, she said that the Winifred Bowen-Davies school has never been involved in anything like this before; having three pupils expelled from a residential course. Apparently, she's already phoned your parents and said she intends to take a very serious view of the matter!' He folded his arms with grim satisfaction, and leaned back against the wall.

Holly tried to ignore him. They had to think of the job in hand, rather than Mike's insults; stealing the diamonds and saving Daniel Martyn. As Mike went off to fetch the Land-rover to take them into town, she turned to whisper to Tracy. 'How do you think he looks?' she asked.

'Who, Mike?'

'Yes. Does he look like someone who's just committed a murder?' She hadn't slept a wink in spite of their early night, fearing for Daniel's safety.

Tracy shivered and took a deep breath. Then she shook her head. 'No. Underneath all that sneering and mocking stuff, I'd say he still looks pretty nervous. And tired,' she added.

'Me too. But we'll soon know.' Belinda looked at her watch. 'When do we meet up with Daniel?'

'Eleven forty-five.' Holly paced up and down the hall. She managed to smile up at Steffie, sitting at the top of the stairs, waiting to wave them off.

Steffie nodded back and pointed at Belinda. 'Très élégante!' she quipped. 'Very smart!'

Belinda patted the coil of hair on top of her head. Though she might not look it, she was ready for action as soon as Mike dropped them off at Windermere bus station.

'Come on, let's go!' Tracy said. 'The sooner we

get this bit over with, the better!' She heard the Land-rover pull up outside the door and heaved her rucksack on to her shoulder.

'Wait just a second!' Holly had taken out the town plan of Windermere to study it one last time. She checked the route from bus station to lakeside. 'I reckon this will take us no more than five minutes,' she calculated. 'If we cut through this alley here, it means we can stay ahead of Mike. He'll have to take the car on this one-way system, through all the traffic!'

Holly and Belinda nodded. 'Pray for a traffic jam!' Belinda said.

Holly folded the map and stuck it into her back pocket as she heard Mike come quickly up the front steps.

'Put the bags in the back,' he ordered. 'I have to go and tell Jo that you're ready to leave.'

They did as they were told, then climbed into the Land-rover. They swallowed hard as Mike emerged with the leader of the centre.

Jo rested one arm on the open back window and looked inside. She seemed sad, rather than angry. 'I've telephoned to arrange things with Miss Horswell,' she told them quietly. 'We agreed that we'd taken the right decision. She thinks that sending you home early will teach you a lesson, so

174

we said we'd meet her halfway, at the bus station in Windermere. She said it was the easiest place for her to find. It's all fixed for twelve o'clock.'

Holly felt her face flush hot. She found she couldn't offer Jo any reply.

'No doubt you had your reasons for behaving like this?' Jo looked at each one of them, paving the way for an explanation even now. They felt Mike bristle as he climbed up into the driver's seat, ready to deny any charges they might make. But they still had no proof, and they were silent. 'Well,' Jo said with a sigh. She stood upright and pushed the door to. 'Perhaps Miss Horswell will be able to get some sense out of you.' She nodded at Mike and turned sadly away.

Mike put the car into gear and eased off down the drive. As Holly turned for a last glimpse of Butterpike Hall, she saw Steffie standing waving them off from under the carved stone entrance.

The mountains and lakes slid by outside the car windows. Boats sailed on clear blue water, islands dotted the sparkling lakes, windsurfers criss-crossed, a water-skier traced a bright white curve on the surface. Mike Sandford sped along the narrow roads, round sharp bends. His jaw was set firm, his hand hovering over the car horn, ready to warn slow drivers out of his way. In the back, Holly, Tracy and Belinda clung to the roll-bars in silence.

He spoke only once on the long journey. They were high in one of the mountain passes, amidst crags and scree. Obviously deciding that he'd nothing to lose, he began to gloat over his victory.

'This is what you get for messing with me,' he told them. 'Playing amateur detective! Spying on me, taking notes, holding secret meetings! You thought you could get away with it!' He slammed his way down the gears, the engine whined up the snaking road. He laughed. 'How does it feel to know you lost?' The car reached the summit and began its dizzying descent into Windermere.

Holly glanced at Tracy and Belinda. They pressed their lips tight shut, refusing to rise to Mike's bait. Soon he would get a shock. Soon they would wipe the smile off his face. They hoped.

The Land-rover followed signs and arrows for the town centre. Pretty gabled houses built from Lakeland stone lined the streets. Hanging baskets full of brick-red geraniums hung from every street lamp. The place was packed with tourists, clogging the narrow streets.

They crawled to a halt. Mike tapped the steering-wheel and glanced impatiently at his watch. Then they crept along again, past gift-shops and stores selling walking boots and outdoor wear. The girls stared out of the windows, trying to get their bearings. It was just past eleven-thirty.

'About time!' Mike spied a sign for the bus station and took a final left turn. He braked into a parking bay to one side of a row of bus shelters.

Holly spotted Miss Horswell standing by the booking-office. With her neatly styled grey hair and dressed in a smart navy suit, she looked every bit the respectable headmistress. 'Ready?' she asked the other two. Their faces told her they were as nervous as she was.

Mike jumped out of the car and strode round to the back door. He flung it open and grabbed Tracy's rucksack. 'You three go and face the music,' he ordered. 'I'll start bringing the bags across.'

Taking deep breaths, they ran across the tarmac. Miss Horswell spotted them and stepped forward. She looked as if she had a speech of disapproval at the ready, lips pursed, head to one side.

'Miss Horswell, we're really sorry!' Holly's breathless, prepared greeting sprang from her lips. 'We can explain everything . . .' She looked up and down the length of the station and spied the Ladies rest room down at the bottom. 'Only, is it OK if we just use the rest room, please?' She appealed in an urgent tone.

Miss Horswell raised her eyebrows, then nodded. 'I suppose so, but be quick. We can't leave Mr Sandford to manage the bags by himself! Go along!'

Holly, Tracy and Belinda sped off down the bus station. But instead of dashing into the rest room as they'd said, they ran straight by. They cut to the right, out of the bottom of the station, and they kept on running. One glance behind showed Miss Horswell's stunned astonishment and Mike Sandford's sudden rage as he realised they'd tricked him one last time. But there was no chance to take it in; Holly led the way down sidestreets towards the lakeside.

They wove in and out of the crowds along the sunny streets. They slipped through stands full of postcards, past stalls selling ice-cream. Holly made sure of the way; down this alley, across that courtyard, remembering it from the town plan. In four minutes flat, they reached the long wooden jetty where the famous old steamboats were moored. Beyond that was the endless stretch of silver-blue water.

'There's the Coffee Pot!' Tracy pointed to a white shop front overlooking the jetty. Its sign showed a shiny brown coffee pot. It was quaint and cosy-looking. Several tables stood outside, looking clean and inviting. Inside, they glimpsed red gingham curtains and clean pine tables.

'So far, so good!' Belinda gasped. 'But where's Daniel?' They searched the shingly beach for any sign of the boy they'd come to save.

'There!' Holly spotted a tall, slim figure in jeans and a blue shirt. He emerged from behind a boatshed by the water, stepping towards them through the swans and children. Holly jumped down from the wooden jetty and ran towards him. She grabbed him by his good arm. 'This is Daniel! Daniel, meet Tracy and Belinda!' She introduced them.

Tracy grinned at him. 'Hey, I've never been so glad to see someone I never met before!'

Belinda smiled too, and tugged at her white blouse to pull it straight after the frantic scramble through the back streets. 'Hi. Any sign of Slingsby and Carter?' she asked.

Daniel nodded. 'They went into the cafe about five minutes ago. I had to keep well out of the way back here, but I'm sure it was them! Where's Mike?' He looked anxiously up and down the flower-lined street which separated the waterfront from the cafe.

'He got a bit caught up at the station!' Holly laughed. Relief at finding Daniel safe gave her confidence to push ahead with their plan. 'Belinda's going to act as waitress and call Carter to the phone,' she told him. 'The idea is to split up the two of them, while we keep the owner busy so she doesn't spot what Belinda's up to. After that, we have to rush Carter for the diamonds.' She turned to Belinda. 'OK?'

Belinda nodded and straightened her skirt.

'Good; we'll be right there with you!' Holly promised. 'Remember, you have to bring Carter out towards the back door! And give us a chance to talk to the cafe owner before you go in with the message. About two minutes should do it. Right?'

Again Belinda nodded. 'Good luck!' she said to everyone, as she cut off round the side of the Coffee Pot. She needed to find a back way, and a chance to slip quietly in.

Holly signalled to Daniel to keep well out of sight of the front window, while she and Tracy sat down at an outside table, waiting to be served. Daniel took cover behind a nearby postcard stand. He kept a wary look out for Mike's Land-rover. But he gave a thumbs-up as Holly and Tracy pressed ahead.

180

After a few seconds a blonde-haired, middle-aged woman in a blue-patterned dress came to serve them. 'Good morning!' She smiled, pencil and pad in hand.

'Hi!' Tracy smiled back. 'Do you have chocolate ice-cream, please?' She made her voice sound more American than usual. She wanted to play the typical tourist. 'This is such a sweet town!' she gushed. 'And your little place is so pretty!'

The woman nodded and smiled. '*Two* chocolate ice-creams, would that be?' She looked at Holly.

Holly took her time to decide. She glanced into the cafe and caught a glimpse of two men sitting hunched over a table. But there was no time to see if Belinda had made it yet, through the back way to deliver the vital message.

Then Tracy came up with another idea. 'Say!' she said to the proprietor. She took a mini-camera out of her pocket and held it up. 'Would you mind taking a picture of me and my friend? I mean, would it be a bother?' She smiled sweetly.

The woman nodded again. 'Not at all.' She put down her notepad and took the camera from Tracy. 'I get asked to do this all the time!' she said. Good-humouredly she put the camera to her eye, ready to click the shutter.

'Smile!' Tracy told Holly, one arm stretched along the back of her seat.

'Wait a sec!' Holly pretended to fix her hair and get into position. The woman stood poised with the camera. Every second counted.

Inside the cafe building, Belinda looked warily along a narrow back corridor. Nearest to her was a glass door leading to a public telephone booth. Then there was a door with a WC sign, and another leading into a kitchen. On the opposite side was a door into the cafe itself. Drawing herself up tall, taking off her glasses and slipping them into her skirt pocket to get herself into role, she took the plunge and walked in.

Tony Carter and Rob Slingsby sat nervously at a corner table. They had full coffee cups in front of them, but they stared intently out of the window at figures passing by. Slingsby crossed his legs and swung the top one to and fro. Carter kept his heavy fingers firmly clasped round a sturdy leather wallet placed on the table next to his coffee cup.

Quickly Belinda took all this in. She advanced towards their table. There were just two other people in the cafe, an elderly couple with a panting black-and-white spaniel at their feet. Tony Carter glanced up as Belinda approached. 'Yes?' he snapped.

He obviously hadn't recognised her. Belinda swallowed hard, thanking her lucky stars. Outside, Tracy and Holly had managed to persuade the cafe owner into taking their photograph. 'Excuse me, sir, I'm sorry to bother you,' she said. 'But are you Mr Carter?'

The man took in a sharp breath. 'So?' he nodded.

'There's a phone message for you from a Mr Mike Sandford,' she told him. 'He'd like to speak to you. He asked me to tell you it's urgent.'

Carter sprang to his feet. His chair tipped back. Without stopping to think, he followed Belinda. 'Where? Which way?' He couldn't get out of the door quickly enough.

'This way, sir.' Belinda led him between the pine tables with their red-checked cloths. She felt him breathing down her neck. When she reached the door, she glanced back to see Slingsby still sitting tight. He chewed his lip and looked anxiously at his watch. Carter bumped into her, half-shoving past her into the back corridor. 'Which way?' he demanded again. 'Where's the phone?'

'This way!' Now Belinda led him down the narrow corridor, just as planned.

But she realised that something had gone horribly wrong. Something vital. In his surprise, Carter

183

had leapt to his feet and pushed the wallet towards Slingsby, who had seized hold of it. The wallet containing the diamonds! How would Holly and the others get at it now?

Slingsby sat in the cafe, guarding the diamonds, uneasy and suspicious at the turn of events. He had one hand firmly on the wallet, ready for anything.

Belinda showed Carter the phone booth at the end of the corridor. She spied Holly, Tracy and Daniel already hovering in the outside doorway, ready to pounce. As Carter disappeared inside the booth, Belinda ran to the door. In a moment, Carter would discover the trick. 'He hasn't got the diamonds!' she whispered frantically to Holly. 'They're still on the table! Slingsby's got them!' Then she dashed back down the corridor.

Carter burst out of the booth, his face furious. 'What's going on here?' he demanded, confronting Belinda. 'This phone's dead! What are you up to?'

'Maybe Mr Sandford got cut off?' Belinda stammered. She must try to cover up for a few moments longer. 'Why not wait to see if he tries to ring back?'

Carter glanced agitatedly at his watch, then back at Belinda.

'He'll probably try again,' she urged.

For the first time, he stared closely at her face. There was a sudden look of recognition. Belinda began to back away.

'Hey, just a minute,' he said, following her into the cafe. 'Haven't I seen you somewhere before?'

15   The snatch

There was chaos in the corridor. Carter pushed Belinda to one side to make his way quickly back into the cafe. At the corner table, Slingsby had sprung to his feet in alarm. The blonde-haired cafe owner hurried in to investigate the disturbance.

No point bothering with Carter, Holly thought. She struggled to keep cool in the sudden emergency. 'It's Slingsby we need to tackle now!' she told Daniel and Tracy. Belinda was still trying to fend off an enraged Carter.

Quick as a flash, Daniel ran round to the front of the cafe. 'This way!' he yelled.

'What's he up to?' Tracy dashed after him. 'He'll get caught if he's not careful! Help me stop him, Holly!'

But Daniel rushed to stand full square in the open doorway of the Coffee Pot. Tracy and Holly followed, watching as Slingsby spun round to face Daniel. He sent coffee cups flying as he lunged forward, seeing the boy standing there large as life.

Slingsby let out an outraged gasp, grabbed the wallet from the table and leapt at Daniel. He charged for the door, but Daniel, Holly and Tracy rushed at him, caught him off balance and wrestled to snatch the diamonds from him.

'Grab them, Daniel!' Holly yelled. She ducked and pulled at Slingsby's jacket to stop him escaping. Tracy dived for his legs.

Daniel grabbed hold of Slingsby's wrist and began to pull at the wallet. Slingsby kicked out at Tracy, but she clung on. Holly still dragged him back. At last they got him on to the floor. The wallet shot out of his hand and went spinning out of reach.

Holly and Daniel sprang after the diamonds. She reached them first. 'I've got them!' she yelled.

'Watch out, Holly!' Belinda warned. Carter had broken free in the back corridor. He spotted Holly.

'Help!' The poor cafe owner stood amidst the confusion. The elderly couple with the spaniel cowered in one corner. 'Somebody help!' she wailed.

Carter crashed into the woman and sent her spinning towards the glass counter. It gave Holly,

Daniel and Tracy the few extra seconds they needed. Leading the way with the wallet, Holly turned and ran.

She made it to the door. As she and Daniel ran through, Tracy slammed it shut behind her. Belinda joined them from the side alley. Together, they made their getaway.

They darted into the road. Traffic squealed to a halt. They heard Slingsby and Carter fling open the cafe door and give chase. Then a grey Land-rover lurched from the stationary cars. It bore down on them across the wide pavement towards the marina. Mike Sandford had caught up with the action at last!

Holly leap-frogged a high concrete flower-tub, clutching the wallet in one hand. She knew Daniel, Tracy and Belinda were still close by. She heard Mike crunch the Land-rover savagely against the flower-tub. Then the door opened. There was an angry shout, more footsteps. 'Keep going!' Holly gasped.

Passers-by stood bewildered. No one moved a muscle, even when Slingsby and Carter ran across the road after them, shouting and yelling. Holly's group came to a sudden halt by the water's edge.

'This way!' Belinda ducked straight under the

188

wooden jetty. Holly, Tracy and Daniel soon followed. 'Four against three!' she cried.

Holly flashed her a triumphant grin. She held up the diamonds.

'Terrific!' Belinda gasped. They headed off along the lapping shore.

'Stop them!' It was Mike Sandford's voice roaring, taking charge of the situation. He swung under the jetty, with Carter and Slingsby close behind. Their heavy footsteps crunched over the pebbles.

People backed off in alarm.

'This way!' Daniel swerved and charged up the beach. He skirted round the back of the watching crowd, kicking up the pebbles as he ran. The girls followed.

Holly still held fast to the wallet as she pushed her way through. She felt the stones crunch under foot. Behind them, the three men tried to follow, but the crowd got in their way, slowing them down.

'We're gaining on them!' Holly gasped.

But Daniel, scrambling up a wall on to the road, pulled to a halt. There were sirens wailing, cars moving to one side to let the police through. Soon the way ahead would be blocked.

'Let's cut back up through the town!' Belinda

189

suggested. Her hair had tumbled down from its neat coil. She was breathless, but determined.

Holly nodded. They leapt up off the pebbles on to the flagged promenade, over the flowerbeds into the road.

Mike Sandford cut diagonally across the beach. He was trying to head her off, gaining ground, as Holly battled through another group of onlookers. She saw the danger. Quickly she glanced sideways and slipped the wallet full of diamonds to Tracy, who caught it like a rugby player streaking down the wing. She side-stepped the crowd and pressed on, Belinda and Daniel alongside.

Mike swerved. He yelled instructions to his accomplices. 'Follow them! They're getting away!'

The crowd gasped and whirled round to watch the escape. Holly slipped through a gap and managed to catch up with the others. They headed past the Coffee Pot, into the network of courtyards and alleys behind.

'Head for the bus station!' Holly yelled. Their feet echoed up a narrow, stone-flagged alleyway, towards a square of gift shops and more cafes. She recognised the route. 'This way!' She slipped down a left-hand turning, out of sight of their pursuers.

'Just keep hold of that wallet, for goodness sake!' Belinda gasped at Tracy.

190

Tracy nodded. Head down, she sprinted across the square towards the station.

Straight into the bulky figure of Mike Sandford! More familiar with the town, he'd cut through a different way and got there first. Tracy cannoned into him and dropped the wallet. It spun open on the ground, threatening to spill its contents far and wide.

Holly gasped and dived to the pavement. She flicked the wallet shut and seized it once more. Mike bent, a moment too late, and made a grab for it. Holly shoved hard against his knees. They buckled. He staggered forwards as she crawled clear.

Then they were off again, Daniel leading the way, Carter bringing up the rear, all seven sprinting for the row of bus shelters in the centre of town.

'Over there!' Belinda pointed to where Miss Horswell still stood, looking bemused and surrounded by rucksacks, talking to a policewoman about three missing girls.

Holding the wallet firmly to her chest, Holly sprinted the final stretch. She arrived breathless but triumphant, and she thrust the stolen diamonds into the hands of the police!

'I said we'd explain later!' Holly half-laughed,

half-cried with relief. Tracy and Belinda had their arms around her shoulders, holding each other up. Daniel studied the sparkling white stones which lay cushioned in the policewoman's palm. His chest heaved. He put his head back and gasped for breath.

'And this is what all the fuss is about?' Miss Horswell tipped a diamond the size of a map-pinhead with her forefinger. It rolled and winked up at them. 'I think I'm just beginning to under-stand!'

The chase had come to an end when Holly thrust the fortune into the policewoman's hands. 'Proof!' she gasped. 'Now no one can say Daniel Martyn is a liar!'

Mike Sandford had stopped dead in his tracks. His face was white, his fists clenched. He'd turned to run. But the police acted swiftly. They rounded him up, together with Slingsby and Carter.

Holly left the explanations to Daniel. He told the police the full story, there in Windermere bus station; the smuggled stones, the false charges, the fatal fall.

More police arrived in their white-and-orange cars, lights flashing. Six or seven officers joined the scene. The policewoman held out the diamonds to show them.

Someone whistled softly. 'They must be worth a fortune!'

Mike Sandford's face twisted into a deep frown. He gritted his teeth. Carter and Slingsby stood behind him, handcuffed, heads bowed.

'Take them away!' a policeman ordered.

Car doors opened and slammed. Gradually the station emptied.

Holly caught a glimpse of Mike Sandford's face as he was driven off. It glared at her through the glass, a stony stare.

Carefully the policewoman rolled the diamonds back into their wallet. She sealed it and handed it over to her superior officer. Then she smiled and turned to Holly, Tracy and Belinda.

'Does this mean Daniel's in the clear?' Holly asked.

The policewoman nodded. 'It certainly looks like it!'

Tracy and Belinda slumped against the wall with relief. Daniel grinned at Holly. 'Is now the time to say thanks?' he asked. 'It sounds a bit feeble, considering!' He shoved his hands in his pockets and blushed deep crimson.

Holly smiled. She felt on top of the world. 'It was worth it!' she told him.

'Every moment!' Tracy grinned.

'Every centimetre of mountain, every second of pain and fear!' Belinda groaned.

'You exaggerate!' Holly told her.

Belinda spread her hands in protest. 'No, I don't! Believe me, Miss Horswell, every word I say is true! And I never want to come on another adventure holiday in my entire life, ever again! Is that clear?'

Back in school uniform, back at her desk in the school magazine office, Holly sighed with satisfaction. She'd been reading through the latest copy of *Winformation*, picking up the headline of an article by Steffie which ran 'Mystery Club Steals Fortune!' Miss Horswell had added her own note of pride and gratitude to the three student detectives of the Winifred Bowen-Davies school.

'"Charges against the three men include receiving stolen goods, smuggling, and attempts to pervert the course of justice." Wow!' Holly read it out loud and looked up at Tracy and Belinda.

Tracy seized the magazine. 'Hey, Belinda, you get a special mention! Listen to this! "Belinda Hayes bravely carried out the role of waitress, to lure Tony Carter away from his accomplice." What do you think?'

194

'Hmm!' Belinda blinked and fixed her glasses firmly on to her nose. She read through the article again. 'It says something else as well. Listen. "Belinda also overcame her terror of heights to carry out an abseiling trick which diverted Mike Sandford's attention while Holly Adams carried out an important rendezvous with fugitive Daniel Martyn."' She read it out slowly, then looked up at Holly and Tracy with a broad smile. 'That doesn't sound too bad, does it?'

'Brilliant!' they agreed, laughing.

Just then, Steffie's head appeared round the door. 'Do you like it?' she asked, pointing to the article in the magazine.

'It's great. Thanks, Steffie,' Holly said with a grin.

'Have you heard how Daniel is?' Steffie came to join them.

'He's back at school. They finally got in touch with his mum and dad. They flew straight over. Everything's fine,' Tracy reported.

'*His* mum wrote *my* mum a thank-you letter,' Belinda told her. 'In fact, she wrote to all of our families to say what great things we'd done for her son!'

Steffie sat at her desk and nodded. 'And what did your mum say?'

Belinda tossed her head and looked at Tracy and Holly. 'How shall I put it? Let's just say she wasn't too pleased.' She blushed at the memory of her mother dashing to pick her up from school on the previous Friday.

'"Oh, Belinda, how could you?"' Tracy put on her Mrs Hayes voice. '"How could you let your father and me down like this?"'

'You're joking!' Steffie stared at Tracy.

'No way. She was in real trouble for a couple of minutes back there, believe me!'

Steffie shook her head.

'Just for a while,' Belinda cheerfully agreed. 'But then Dad got out of the car and told the Mystery Club to climb in the back. He said everyone had to follow him down to his favourite Italian restaurant; Holly's lot and Tracy's mum.' A smile crept across her face at the memory. 'We all piled into the cars and went straight downtown for pizzas . . .'

'And ice-cream!' Tracy drooled.

'Chocolate ice-cream!' Holly reminded them.

Belinda sighed. 'And we all lived happily ever after!'

Holly and Tracy grinned. 'Until the next time,' Tracy agreed.

'Never again!' Belinda insisted. 'Wild horses wouldn't drag me back to Butterpike Hall!'

'No, she means until we're faced with our next mystery, don't you, Tracy?' Holly gave a laugh. 'We'll live happily ever after – until the next mystery comes along for us to solve!'

Another Hodder Children's book

**DARK HORSE
THE MYSTERY CLUB 11**

Fiona Kelly

Holly stepped forward to close the
stable door. Suddenly, she heard
footsteps behind her. Before she could
turn, someone gave her a hard shove.
She pitched forward and the door was
slammed and bolted behind her.

Holly was trapped!

There's a horse thief on the loose and
Holly is a witness to his crimes – but the
police don't believe her! Then Meltdown
disappears and it's up to Holly, Belinda
and Tracy – The Mystery Club – to trap
the thief.

Another Hodder Children's book

DECEPTIONS
THE MYSTERY CLUB 12

Fiona Kelly

Tracy barely heard the car approaching
from behind her bike. By the time she
realised something was wrong, it was
too late. The car struck her knee and she
struggled desperately to keep her balance.
A moment later the wheels slid from
under her . . .

P. J. Benson, the mystery writer, has
promised Holly an interview. But when
they meet Holly is in for a shock! Why
is the writer behaving so strangely? And
why does she insist on secrecy? Holly,
Belinda and Tracy – The Mystery Club
– set out to unravel the web of lies and
deceit . . .

Another Hodder Children's book

SPY-CATCHERS!
THE MYSTERY KIDS 1

Fiona Kelly

London is teeming with spies – and Holly
Adams and Miranda Hunt are just the
people to catch them. All they need is
practice. Who is the sinister man lurking
outside Holly's house in the dead of
night? What does Miranda's mum *really*
do for the government?

Then they spot a suspicious-looking boy –
and the real mystery begins . . .

Another Hodder Children's book

LOST AND FOUND
THE MYSTERY KIDS 2

Fiona Kelly

Holly's desperate for a mystery to solve –
and when she sees a ferrety-looking man
throw his wallet from the bus, she knows
she's found one!

Miranda and Peter aren't so sure. The
wallet is empty when they go back to
find it. Empty except for some sort of
ticket – and there's nothing mysterious
about that.

Or is there . . .?

THE MYSTERY CLUB SERIES
FIONA KELLY

58867 5	SECRET CLUES	£2.99
58868 3	DOUBLE DANGER	£2.99
58869 1	FORBIDDEN ISLAND	£2.99
58870 5	MISCHIEF AT MIDNIGHT	£2.99
59283 4	DANGEROUS TRICKS	£2.99
59284 2	MISSING!	£2.99
60723 8	HIDE AND SEEK	£3.50
60724 6	BURIED SECRETS	£3.50
60725 4	DEADLY GAMES	£3.50
60726 2	CROSSED LINES	£3.50
60727 0	DARK HORSE	£3.50
60728 9	DECEPTIONS	£3.50

All these books are available at your local bookshop or newsagent or can be ordered direct from the publisher. Just tick the titles you want and fill in the form below.

Prices and availability subject to change without notice.

HODDER AND STOUGHTON PAPERBACKS, PO Box 11, Falmouth, Cornwall.

Please send cheque or postal order for the value of the book, and add the following for postage and packing.
UK including BFPO – £1.00 for the book, plus 50p for the second book, and 30p for each additional book ordered up to a £3.00 maximum.
OVERSEAS INCLUDING EIRE – £2.00 for the first book, plus £1.00 for the second book and 50p for each additional book ordered.
OR Please direct debit this amount from my Access/Visa Card (delete as appropriate).

Card Number

Amount £ ....

Expiry Date ....

Signed ....

Name ....

Address ....